CUM FOR ME VOLUME 5

Touch Me, Tease Me

Lock Down Publications & Ca$h Whispers
Cum For Me 5
A Collection of Erotic Tales

.

Lock Down Publications
P.O. Box 870494
Mesquite, Tx 75187

Visit our website at **www.lockdownpublications.com**

First Edition August 2019
Printed in the United States of America
This is a work of fiction. Names, characters, places, and incidents either are products of the author's imagination or are used fictitiously. Any similarity to actual events or locales or persons, living or dead, is entirely coincidental.
Cover design and layout by: Dynasty's Cover Me
Book interior design by: Shawn Walker
Edited by: Jill Alicea

Stay Connected with Us!

Text **LOCKDOWN** to 22828 to stay up-to-date with new releases, sneak peaks, contests and more…

Thank you!

Submission Guideline.

Submit the first three chapters of your completed manuscript to ldpsubmissions@gmail.com, subject line: Your book's title. The manuscript must be in a .doc file and sent as an attachment. Document should be in Times New Roman, double spaced and in size 12 font. Also, provide your synopsis and full contact information. If sending multiple submissions, they must each be in a separate email.

Have a story but no way to send it electronically? You can still submit to LDP/Ca$h Presents. Send in the first three chapters, written or typed, of your completed manuscript to:

LDP: Submissions Dept
Po Box 870494
Mesquite, Tx 75187

DO NOT send original manuscript. Must be a duplicate.

Provide your synopsis and a cover letter containing your full contact information.

Thanks for considering LDP and Ca$h Presents.

These stories are brought to you by Destiny Skai.
Enjoy them!

GUERILLA DICK ZO

KENNEDI

Here I was sitting in my office, once again, disappointed with the results of the numerous amount of untalented bastards to grace my presence during auditions. Everybody wanted to be famous, but lacked the skills needed in this industry. I am a New York Times bestseller in urban fiction and I direct movies. So yes, I am the female Tyler Perry in the game. All I needed was the main character and then I could begin filming. I laid my head on my desk and shed a few tears. I was beyond frustrated, which was why I sent my personal assistant home for the day. Times like this I wish my husband was still alive. He passed away eight months ago in a motorcycle accident and I've been lost ever since. I buried myself in my work to keep my sanity and to fill the loneliness in my heart. The battle was real, so I shot a quick prayer to the man upstairs and asked him to bring closure to my needs. No sooner had I said amen than my thoughts were interrupted by a baritone voice.

"Excuse me, am I late for the auditions?"

I rolled my eyes because I was not in the mood for any more disappointments. All I wanted to do was start fresh the next morning and find some fresh talent. I slowly raised my head.

"Sorry, but you have to come - "

I stopped mid-sentence because standing in front of me was the finest piece of eye candy I'd seen in a while. This man was 5'11" with brown skin, chestnut brown eyes, nice teeth, and waves that were deep as my pussy. My clit thumped just from the sound of his voice. Sex in my world was non-existent, so of course he had me on ten with no effort.

"Um. Actually. You." Listen to myself sounding like a fool, stumbling on my words and shit. He just stood there, awaiting a solid answer from me.

"I apologize. What I'm trying to say is that you can still audition. Grab the script on that table and let me see what you got."

With no hesitation, he grabbed one of the scripts and gave it all he had. The man was a natural. In order to make sure he could adapt in any situation, I tested him by making him read a sex scene with some very nasty dialogue. Before he started reading the lines, he licked his lips seductively, and that shit sent a tingle down my spine. I rocked my leg in an effort to cool down the fire that was transpiring between my legs. He would've had a bitch ready to come out of my La Perla draws if I had been wearing them.

"Get on your knees and suck this dick. I want you to catch all my babies on that pretty little face of yours." With a devilish grin he looked up and laughed. "Should I continue?"

"Yes, but this time I want you to act it out with me. I'm going to feed you the lines." I grabbed the master copy of the script from the corner of my desk and stood up.

"That would probably be best."

His eyes followed my every move until I was standing in front of my desk. Something told me that he was intrigued by my sex appeal. The Chanel dress I was rocking hugged my body tight and in all the right places. I leaned against my desk. "I'll start."

"Let's do it." He smiled.

"Cameron, I thought you were dead." I looked into his eyes deeply, as if he was the love of my life. "They found your car with blood in it and I thought I lost you forever."

"Yeah, I got shot, but that wasn't shit. I had to lay low for a while, but I'm back now." He stepped closer to me, pulling me close to him, and kissed the side of my neck, just as the script instructed him to do. However, I wasn't prepared for that or the scent of his hypnotizing cologne.

"Get on your knees and suck this dick. I want you to catch all my babies on that pretty little face of yours."

When he looked up, he must've peeped the look on my face and gotten the wrong idea. "I'm sorry. Did I go too far?"

"No. That was good, thank you. You're a natural." I wasn't upset, to say the least, and to be honest, we could've gone further, but I knew I needed to remain professional.

"Thank you." He smiled.

"I'm sorry, what's your name?"

"Lorenzo, but my friends call me Zo."

"So you consider me a friend already?" I couldn't resist flirting with his sexy ass.

Lorenzo licked those pink-ass lips again. "You could be."

"Here, have a seat and lets discuss your new role."

"Word? I got the role?"

"If you want it."

"That's not a question, because I wouldn't be here if I didn't." Lorenzo held his arm out. "No disrespect, of course."

"None taken." I headed over to my mini-fridge, where I kept Hennessey on deck after long days and nights. "Would you like a drink?"

"It depends on what it is."

I pulled the bottle from the fridge and held it in the air. "Hennessey."

"Yeah, I'll have one."

I poured each of us a drink and we made a toast. "To new beginnings."

"To new beginnings," he repeated.

Lorenzo and I sat and talked for two hours and we were good and tipsy. During that time, I learned that he was single and he didn't have any kids. That was a bonus because I was childless myself. But here was the kicker: he was only twenty-one and I had just celebrated my thirty-second birthday. At that moment, I felt like age was nothing but a number because I was intoxicated by this young man. I walked over to the opposite side of my desk where he was seated and hopped up on it. I knew what I wanted, and I wanted it fast and hard. Deep down inside, I was happy that I had shaved that morning and worn a skirt. Opening my legs wide, I gave him a peek at my bare pussy, since I wasn't a fan of panties.

Lorenzo gripped his dick and stood up quickly as he walked over to me. "Is this a scene in the movie that I should practice for?"

My eyes were glued to the big bulge in his pants. He was swinging heavy to be so young. It made me wonder what his mama had fed him as a baby. I'm sure it was the hormones in the milk. I placed my hand

11

in between my legs and rubbed my clit. "It could be." I purred like a kitten.

Standing in front of me, he positioned himself between my legs and pushed my skirt up to my waist. Zo was aggressive when he ripped my fishnet stockings off. That instantly sent my body into shock, along with aggressive tidal waves against my vaginal walls. He licked the side of my neck, stopping to suck on it a little.

A slight moan crept from my mouth. "Mm."

Then my hands made a beeline for his belt buckle. This man was driving me insane and all I wanted was his stiff dick to penetrate these tight-ass virgin walls. "Fuck me right now!" I demanded.

Zo chuckled a bit. "Patience, baby, you gon' get the dick, I promise."

"You got me so horny."

"I know. And when I get in it, I'ma kill this pussy."

I could feel one of his fingers gliding its way inside my moist, throbbing nookie. Then he eased two more in and plunged deep inside, finger fucking me fast. I gyrated my hips like I was fucking him. I tilted my head back and closed my eyes while biting my bottom lip.

My heart dropped to the crack of my ass when he grabbed my legs, snatching me towards him, and forced my legs behind my head. Sloppily, he tongue kissed my swollen pearl and nibbled on it gently with his teeth. My body trembled and I wanted to snatch my hair out of my head. Instead, I placed my hands on his head and pushed his head further down while grinding against his mouth. I needed the full effect of that dome. He ate my pussy until I came all over his juicy, full lips and the stubble on his chin.

Zo released my legs and licked his lips. "I need you face down."

The bass in his voice had a bitch at attention and anxious to see what he was about to deliver. I got up fast and positioned myself on my desk while he removed his shirt and tossed it onto the floor. My stomach was resting on my desk with my ass facing him.

"Put your leg up."

I did like I was told and put one leg on the desk and one on the floor.

Zo eagerly slipped his dick inside of me from the back and hammered my pussy. He was rough with it, but that was exactly what I wanted.

"Fuck me." I moaned loud like I was possessed while spreading my cheeks to give him a clear shot of my creamy, bald center. The gushy, smacking sound echoed throughout the room as his pelvis crashed violently against my ass. We were the only ones left in the building, so we could be as loud as we wanted without being caught.

"You like this young dick, don't you?" he boasted.

"Fuck yeah."

Zo wasn't a rookie by a long shot. He had a tight grip on my chin as he pulled my head back towards him and stuck his fingers in my mouth. My juices were sweet like nectar due to the healthy vegan lifestyle that I had chosen for the last four months. The only meat I was interested in eating was his dick when my chance came around.

"Ah. Sss. Ah." His fingers were still in my mouth, but the way his dick was digging in my guts and scrambling my eggs, I couldn't keep quiet. With my arms stretched out, I grabbed the edge of the desk and held on to that shit tight while throwing it back.

Zo finally pulled his fingers from my mouth and inserted a thumb in my ass. He fucked me slowly in both holes and I continued to throw it back. The shit he was doing to me was giving me so much life, and not once did I regret giving up the ass with no effort. His young ass was definitely worth it.

"Throw that ass back." He grunted. "Yeah. Ohhh. This pussy feel so good I gotta taste it."

Zo pulled his dick out, but he continued to fuck me with his thumb and suck my pussy from behind.

"Shit, yeah." I exhaled deeply.

His wet tongue made a trail from my lips all the way north. He rolled his tongue up and down the crack of my ass and I damn near lost it. Zo was licking and slurping and I was enjoying every moment of it. I swear I could fuck him forever. The tongue was everything, but I wanted that meat back inside me. I rolled over onto my back and slid my hand between my legs and played with myself.

"Give me that dick," I demanded.

Destiny Skai

Zo, in turn, listened to me and stuffed his big black summer sausage back inside my tight hole.

"Shit."

And just like that, we were back humping like jack rabbits.

Never in all my years of living did I think I would back track and fuck with someone eleven years my junior, but I knew for a fact that he was putting some grown men to shame. My life had been completely on hold in the relationship department, since I was still grieving the loss of my soulmate. However, I knew that one day I would have to get back out there. It was what he would want me to do and besides, my body needed the therapy it was receiving. I was tired of playing with pinky, my vibrator.

"Ooh yeah. Fuck." He had my legs spread wide open and the vivid picture of his chocolate dick going in and out of me was a beautiful sight to see. My lips were gripped around his piece tight with every thrust.

"I told you I was gon' kill this pussy, didn't I?"

"Yes. Yes." My mouth was wide open, gasping for air.

Zo beat my back out for another twenty minutes and I couldn't front, but he was wearing my ass out. According to the clock on the wall, we had been at it for damn near an hour and I needed something to drink.

"I'm 'bout ta bust. Fuck." He grunted while thrusting in and out of me mid speed before pulling out his dick and spewing sperm all over my stomach. "Shit. Grrr."

Zo let his limp member fall freely from his hand and kissed me in the mouth. When we came up for air, he looked me in the eyes. "I hope you enjoyed this as much as I did."

Using my right hand, I wiped my bottom lip slowly with pure seduction in my eyes. "Of course I did," I said, then I rubbed his hard chest. "Hopefully this won't be the last time."

"Not if you don't want it to be."

"I could get used to this."

"Believe me, you ain't seen nothing yet."

"Take one of my business cards and call me."

"Okay."

14

After Lorenzo got dressed, he kissed me once more and left my office. I went into the bathroom and washed up in the sink with a huge smile on my face.

On my way home I went by Chick-fil-a to get something to eat. I hadn't eaten all day and I had definitely worked up an appetite. My Na-Na was happy as hell, but my stomach was a little upset. The orgasm he gave me was everything and I couldn't stop smiling. By the time I pulled up into my driveway, it was a little after seven o'clock. Quickly grabbing my items, I locked the doors on my Range Rover truck and rushed into the house. All I wanted was to eat my food, shower, and have a nice night cap that consisted of a blunt and a glass of Hennessey.

Two hours later, I sat at my personal bar in the den, smiling at all of my accomplishments. I had truly come a long way from where I used to be, and I was truly grateful. Over the last two years I was able to gross one million dollars in book sales, produce my first movie, and build a two-story, five bedroom home from the ground up with an Olympic-sized pool in the back, Jacuzzi, and exercising room.

When my drink was finished, I went into the master bedroom, climbed up on my king-sized sleigh bed, and laid there in silence, which was something I hated. Around this time my home was supposed to be filled with kids, but because I wanted to work on my career first, starting a family had been put on the backburner. Now I was regretting the fact that I didn't have a baby with my husband before his untimely demise.

Precious thoughts of him brought tears to my eyes, although I knew he was in a better place. My only issue was there was no one here to carry on his name or legacy, and that was my fault. All I had were memories, pictures, a few home videos, and our wedding footage.

The sudden sound of my cell phone got my attention. I wasn't going to pick it up at first, but I changed my mind since it was only a text message. The name on the screen alone dried my tears instantly and put a girlish smile on my face. It was none other than Guerilla Dick Zo.

Zo: Hey beautiful it's me. I hope you sleep well tonight
Kennedi: I will indeed thanks to you
Zo: Don't stroke my ego
Kennedi: Oh I can do more than stroke your ego lol
Zo: We'll see about that lol
Kennedi: Yes we will
Zo: Goodnight beautiful. I'll see you tomorrow
Kennedi: Goodnight

Snuggling against my pillow with a smile on my face, I closed my eyes. Erotic thoughts about my new boy toy floated in my mind like alphabet soup. Normally at night all I could think about was work and different ways to increase my wealth, but after the day I had, it was hard to focus.

Another notification came through my phone, so I picked it up and opened the message. Zo had sent me a dick picture with the caption, "Dream about us tonight". After masturbating to his photo and creaming on my fingertips, I fell asleep with ease.

***

The following day, I got up with an extra pep in my step and prepared for a long day of rehearsals. Since my new piece of eye candy was in attendance, I wore something special underneath my sleeveless V-neck sheath gray dress. My silver strap-up stiletto heels complimented my attire and bowlegs. My walk was a lot sexier with heels on and I wanted to make sure he peeped the extra swing in my pleasantly plump ass. Over the past few months I had picked up a few extra pounds, but I got that off quick in my home gym. I was the epitome of a brown-skinned bombshell.

On my way to my studio, I stopped by Dunkin Donuts to get a Caramel Iced Latte, a Box O' Joe, and two dozen donuts for my crew. I needed everyone to be on point and ready to work. Filming was set to start in two weeks and we had our work cut out for us.

When I pulled up in the parking lot, my assistant Tia was standing outside awaiting my arrival. She scurried to my truck with a cart and opened the door.

"Good morning, Boss Lady, how are you today?" Tia said cheerfully.

"I'm great, and you?" I handed her the donuts and coffee.

"I'm good."

"Is everyone here? And were they on time?" This was a place of business and I had no problem with deducting their pay.

"Yes, they were." She smiled. "I also see we have a new face. When did you find him?"

"Yesterday after I sent you home, he showed up at the last minute." I grabbed my purse and latte and climbed out of my vehicle.

"Oh, well that's good. We have all the talent we need."

"Yes, we do."

Tia was my first cousin and when I started the business, she had always been supportive of me, even when I couldn't pay her in the beginning. Now that I was on top, she was finally reaping the fruits of her labor. There were plenty of days I wanted to quit, but she gave me that extra push I needed and talked me off the ledge. I loved her for that and as long as I was breathing, she would be fully taken care of.

The room was noisy when I walked in, but it was obvious they were reading through their lines, which is something I appreciated. My team was dedicated to being successful and loyal, to say the least. Whatever I asked of them, they did it. Some were late from time to time, but that was a work in progress, and I believed we finally had that under control.

"Good morning, everyone," I spoke loudly over their voices. "I'm glad to see you working without me."

All twelve of them paused and looked in my direction. "Good morning, Boss Lady."

"Grab your donuts, coffee, and whatever else you need. We'll begin in about twenty minutes."

"Okay!" Charmaine shouted and dropped her script in the chair she was sitting in. The rest of the crew followed suit, including Lorenzo.

I needed a few moments to get situated, so I went into my office and closed the door. Not even a minute later, there was a light tap on the door.

"Come in!" I shouted.

The door crept open and in walked Lorenzo with his sexy ass. There was a huge grin on his face as he closed the door behind him.

"I hope I'm not interrupting, but I thought I would come in and give you a personal hello." He was relaxed as he strolled in my direction, licking his lips. "You looking real edible right about now."

I tried to keep my composure to keep from creaming in the seat of my panties. "Thank you. I take pride in my appearance."

"Oh, I can tell." Lorenzo stood in front me and I couldn't help but become hypnotized by the tantalizing scent of his cologne.

"You smell good." I took in his scent.

"Thank you." Zo groped my ass and kissed my mouth aggressively.

His mouth covered mine, but I managed to mumble, "Not now. I don't want anyone to walk in." Tia had a bad habit of busting in my office from time to time.

"Don't worry; I locked the door." Zo picked me up and sat me on the desk. "I tried to keep it together, but I couldn't resist you."

His strong hands raised my dress and pushed my legs apart with ease so his thick fingers could stroke my thumping crotch. Pushing my panties to the side, he parted my lips and rubbed my clit in a circular motion. My pussy was so wet and I had allowed him to go too far to stop. Zo unzipped his pants as we continued to lock lips, freeing his erection. The force of his dick as it parted my lips took my breath away.

"Fuck." I bit down on my lip. This was certainly not what I had in mind for breakfast, but I couldn't deny my body what it lacked.

Zo thrust in and out of my pussy and held on to the back of my neck, licking me up and down. I held my head back and enjoyed the moment.

"No passion marks please," I moaned softly.

With his free hand, he gripped my ass to keep me in place. Zo rocked his hips back and forth slowly and every now and then he would grind hard against me before digging deep, hitting the bottom. My G spot was going crazy and I was ready to nut all over his dick.

"Go faster."

The sensation against my clit made my legs weak, so I wrapped them around his waist and matched his thrusts. A few minutes later, my insides started to quiver and my volcano was erupting hard as fuck and it was difficult to keep quiet. Zo placed his hand over my mouth to muffle the sounds and hammered away at my pussy.

"Sss. Yeah. Yeah." His voice was low, and of course I commended him for keeping his grunts at a minimum.

Meanwhile, my ass was struggling. The gushy sound of wet smacking was finally coming to a close as the trembles took over his body and slowed down his strokes.

"Damn." He grunted once more and pulled out. "I tried to pull out, but I couldn't."

I heard him loud and clear, but I didn't respond. After work I would be swinging by the pharmacy to grab a Plan B pill. There would be no babies on my watch.

The twenty minutes were almost over, and so was our quickie. I walked over to my desk and grabbed a pack of wipes that I kept stashed. I handed Zo a few and we both cleaned up and fixed our clothes.

"You okay? Did I upset you?" It was obvious he was concerned with my silence, but I was absolutely fine.

"Yeah I'm good. Actually, I'm more than good." To make sure he knew that, I pulled him close to me and slipped my tongue into his mouth. Then I pecked him on the lips. "Keep that same energy for after rehearsal."

"My stamina will always be ready for you." He winked.

"Good. You ready?"

"Yeah."

When we stepped outside the office, the cast was standing around talking, not paying attention. I was happy that everyone was in their own world.

"Okay everyone, let's get ready to begin. Whoever is in the first scene, please take the stage and remember, as you read, make sure you are physically acting out your part. This is the time to get everything down pat so when those cameras are shining brightly, you are comfortable."

The actors took their places on stage while I took a seat in the Director's chair. "When you hear 'action', begin your lines and do not stop until you hear me say cut."

"If we mess up, do you want us to continue?" Charmaine asked, looking in my direction for confirmation.

"Yes. Only stop if I say cut."

"Okay," she replied.

"Action!" I shouted and watched as my book unfolded before my eyes and came to life. Many of the scenes came from my very own personal experiences in life – good and bad, but that was my therapy in getting the word out and spreading awareness all while entertaining. I knew that somewhere in the world I'd touched on a person's current and past situation.

Charmaine was my number one star and main character in the film and on a daily basis, she worked her ass off. The girl was a natural by far, and the chemistry on stage between her and Zo was crazy, yet superb. However, I caught him taking a glimpse at me when things got a little heated between them.

"Cut!" I shouted, interrupting a sensual scene. They both came to a halt. "Zo, when you look at Charmaine, I need you to grab her face and look into her eyes like you love her."

"Got it. I'm ready."

"Action."

"I'm sorry for disappearing when you told me about the baby." Zo grabbed Charmaine's face tenderly and looked deeply into her eyes. "I was afraid, but I promise I'll be here for you until the clock of time runs out."

Charmaine was deep into her role as she became emotional at the drop of a dime. "You hurt me deep with your words. How could I ever trust you again?"

"I'll prove it to you."

"How are you going to do that?" She was able to muster up some tears and they began to fall.

"Like this." Zo slowly got down on one knee and grabbed her hand. "Trinity, I love you and I want to be with you forever. Baby, what I'm saying is, will you marry me?"

"Baby, is this real?"

"Just as sure as I'm on my knees asking for your forgiveness." He paused and just stared at her. "So what's it going to be?"

"Yes. Yes, baby, I will marry you!" she screeched.

"Cut!" I screamed and clapped my hands. "That was excellent. The momentum and love was there, so keep that up and learn your lines by heart. Thank you, and I'll see you all tomorrow."

Rehearsal was nothing short of amazing. We'd managed to scout some awesome talent over an extended period of time and now it was official. I was certainly about to put Broward County on the map with the movie industry. Lorenzo was amazing, on and off the stage, and I couldn't wait until we were alone once again.

Tia walked up to me with a cheesy grin on her face.

"What are you smiling about?" I asked out of curiosity.

"You, girl."

"What do you mean?"

"You like that young boy?" One thing about it: Tia was nosy as they came and loved to sip, spill, and boil any type of tea. We were close and all, but my dealings with Zo were something that I had to keep to myself.

"No, I don't. Why do you think that?"

"Oh." She seemed disappointed. "I thought you did because of how you were looking at him."

"I'm amused by his talent, that's all. He's a natural and exactly what I need from a person with the leading role." I hopped down from my seat. "Stop thinking so much."

In a hurry, I rushed into my office and booked a room online at the Hilton. It was my favorite spot and I accumulated reward points whenever I traveled. But today was different. I wasn't traveling. Once I had the info, I shot a quick text to Zo so he would know what our plan was.

Kennedi: Meet me at the Hilton by the beach in one hour
Zo: I'll be there with bells on
Kennedi: Lol…okay

All I could do was smile at the phone and as usual, Tia walked in without knocking. "Hey, I'm headed out. Do you need anything from me?"

"No. I'm actually headed out myself."

"Well, let's go."

I snatched up my belongings, turned off the office light, and walked out with Tia. Majority of the cast was gone for the day, but some were still lingering around, so I called them out.

"Y'all don't have to go home, but you have to get out of here." I was smiling, but I was dead-ass serious. It was time to go and I had somewhere to be and someone to do.

The remaining members walked out with us and I locked up the studio.

"I'll see you all tomorrow!" I shouted before getting in my truck and backing out. My first stop was to Walgreen's to get a Plan B tablet and then I was on my way.

***

When I pulled up, I didn't know what type of car to look for since I didn't know what he drove to begin with. Just as I was about to call him, I spotted Zo getting out of a Lexus and power-walking in my direction. I laughed when I saw an overnight Louis Vuitton bag draped on his shoulder. On my face were a pair of oversized shades, just in case I was recognized. My personal business was private, and that was the way I planned on keeping it.

Zo opened my door and grabbed my hand. "Very prompt, I see."

"When I say a time, I stick to it." I stepped from my Range Rover. "I see you brought an overnight bag."

"I hope you brought one too." He leaned forward and whispered in my ear, purposely licking it in the process. "When I get finished with you, I promise you'll be too tired to move."

"I did, but is that a threat?"

"It's a promise." Zo grabbed my bag from the backseat and closed the door. "After you, my lady."

The hotel lobby was quiet and I was happy about that. I was able to check in and disappear to the fourth floor undetected. My city loved to gossip and I didn't want to be caught up in the tabloids with a young man just yet - or at all, for that matter. When we made it up to the room, I couldn't wait to take off my heels and unwind for a little bit. I sat down on the bed and leaned forward to unfasten them, but Zo grabbed my hand.

"Leave them on for me."

"I need to shower first."

"I'll be the judge of that." Zo kneeled down in front of me and got on his knees, then eased both hands up my chocolate thighs and pushed them apart. He lowered his head between my legs and inhaled my scent. "Smells good to me."

Zo licked the inside of my thighs, teasing me with his powerful tongue. Of course that made me squirm, but I couldn't move that much because of my dress. I was stuck, so I tried wiggling it up to my waist, but he stopped abruptly.

"Take it off."

I stood up and turned my back to him so he could unzip me. Once I was free, I slipped it over my short curly hair and tossed it on the dresser. Zo took a step back and looked me up and down.

"Damn! I didn't know you was stacked like that." He licked his lips, admiring the all-black lace lingerie set I wore just for him.

"That's because you've never seen me naked."

Zo removed his shirt, tank top, and loosened his belt buckle, allowing his pants to fall to the floor. His hammer was at attention, threatening to bust a hole through his boxers at any moment. My mouth was agape, yet watery as he stood there dripping in his own chocolate. I could tell that he worked out. Zo pulled his boxers down and his dick sprung up, hitting his belly button.

The moment that I dreamed about previously had finally presented itself. I was horny as fuck and ready to get it in. Instead of waiting on Zo to take the lead, I grabbed his dick, signaling him to come closer, and then I licked the shaft. It had been a while since I sucked dick, but that shit was like riding a bike. Once you learn it, you never lose it. I wrapped my lips around the fat tip and sucked on it slowly to savor the taste. Bobbing my head back and forth, I deep throated my first piece of meat until I felt it come in contact with my tonsils, causing me to gag a bit. My mouth was wet as I savored the taste of his pre-cum.

"Fuck yeah. Slurp on that dick." Zo grabbed a handful of my hair and massaged my scalp. That influenced me to suck him off faster at a rapid pace. "Slow down, baby. Make love to that dick. We ain't in no rush."

Zo guided my head at the pace he wanted me to go, which was slow and sensual. That wasn't a problem, so I did it just the way he wanted it.

"Shit. You trying to make me nut fast." Zo backed up, pulling his rod from the grip of my jaws. "Back up on the bed."

Now I was about to see what he meant when he said I hadn't seen nothing yet. I scooted to the middle of the bed, legs cocked open and all. Whatever he had planned, I was ready. Zo climbed up in the bed with that Guerilla Dick pointing in my direction like it was ready to murder some shit. He kneeled between my legs and pushed them far away from each other. One was at twelve o'clock and the other was at the three position like on the clock. This time he didn't waste any time bussing me open and stuffing every inch into my slippery tunnel, pushing deep until I felt his balls smack against my ass.

The discomfort at the bottom of my stomach made me want to holler right off the back, but I held it in. Zo pulled out slowly and pushed it back in.

"Hell yeah, I'ma take my time with this pussy."

Zo stroked my pussy slowly, but he was only putting it in halfway. Thrusting my hips forward, I tried meeting him halfway, but I felt like he was teasing me.

"Go deeper," I moaned.

"You know I am."

He picked up his pace and went deep with it. Rapid movements of his dick going in and out of me made me feel like I was in heaven. His horsepower was on point and he was riding me hard.

"Sss. Ooh. Sss. Ooh."

"Grind with me, baby." He grabbed my ankle and put my toes in his mouth. No man had ever sucked my toes before and I had to admit that I liked it. The level of intensity flowing from my foot to my pussy was something I had never experienced before.

Our thrusts matched one another and we made beautiful erotic music. Zo moved my foot from his mouth and held my leg straight up. The fight between his dick and my pussy was aggressive and one of them was losing the battle. He was hitting every corner, scraping against my walls. Then he hit that one area that got me loose.

"Shit, my G-spot. My G-spot. Don't move. Keep going." Patting my pussy, I rubbed her to get her prepared for the orgasm that was threatening to erupt.

***

Zo

"Move them hips. Fuck me back."

Kennedi was going crazy while I was digging deep in them guts. My plan was to murder that pussy and have that ass sprung. Her shit was tight and good. I could tell that she ain't been fucked in a minute.

She was in good hands now 'cause I was gon' paint her ass every chance she gave me. My dick was massive for my age and I knew she underestimated me because I was younger than her, but she was eating them thoughts and words. Age was nothing but a number 'cause in the bedroom I was a grown-ass, experienced man and I had her weak.

"I'm cumming. I'm cumming."

My dick was coated with her creamy pussy juices. I played with her clit with my thumb and coached her right into a nut.

"Fuck this dick. Give it to me." I put her leg on my shoulder and dug deeper in that pussy. I could feel her walls shake and vibrate on my dick at the same. The constant banging of my dick to her insides made her pussy cry like a newborn baby.

"Say my name." I pinched her clit and shook it gently. Kennedi's eyes rolled to the back of her head like she had come face to face with her maker. Technically she was dead after the way I delivered on my promise and murdered that pussy.

"Zo. Ah. Zo. Ah. I'm cumming."

"Let it go. Bust on this dick." Kennedi came long and hard. The juices flowed freely down the crack of her ass onto the bed. "Hell yeah, that's what I'm talking about."

Once I made sure she got her nut first, it was time to get mine. "Lay on your stomach and put that ass in the air."

Kennedi followed my instructions and turned over. That pussy was fat and looked amazing from the back. I pulled on my dick before I separated her lips with the head. As soon as I made it past the entrance, I went balls deep in that twat. Her back raised up, but I placed my hand on the middle of it and pushed her back down onto the bed. I loved the way her pussy gripped my dick so tight and locked down on it like vice grips.

"Damn, this pussy fie." I squeezed both cheeks and went bananas in it. Felt like I was playing golf. A hole in one. My dick drilled that pretty pink center with no remorse. Every scream that fell upon my ears made me go harder. I wasn't stopping until I caught me a nut. Every time I shoved my dick in, I saw nothing put pretty brown lips and when I pulled out, the pink came with it like it was playing peek-a-boo wit' a nigga.

"I can feel it in my stomach." Kennedi had the sheets gripped tight in her hands.

"You can take it." I smacked her on the ass. "Throw that ass back for me."

"I can't move."

I smacked her on the ass again. "What I said? Throw that ass back."

Kennedi didn't move and since she didn't, I applied more pressure by standing up on my feet and grand slamming my monstrous dick down in her juicy pussy. I fucked her hard like a dog while holding her hips to keep her in place. I was in a zone and my main focus was on catching a nut. She had hers and now it was my turn.

"Shit. You killing me." She was trying to lay down, but I wasn't having that.

"Argh! Fuck. Be still and stop trying to lay down." I grabbed her stomach and held her up. "Give me that pussy."

"Ahhh. Ouuu. Ahhh."

Kennedi couldn't handle the dick. I laughed on the inside when she pulled a pillow to her face and started biting it like that was gon' help her out.

"I ain't no li'l boy, am I?"

She screamed into the pillow, but that didn't answer my question, so I drilled harder. "Who's a little boy?"

"Nobody."

"I didn't think so." The nut that I had been holding was ready to bust through, so I had to free it. I pulled my dick out. "Turn over and suck this dick."

Kennedi rolled over so I could straddle her chest. Opening her mouth, she polished my knob with no hands and I was slightly impressed. My dick started to throb in her mouth, so I pulled it out and ejaculated on her lips and face. At first she licked her lips, but then she acted as if she was drowning in a sea of cum.

"You put that shit in my eye." She used the sheet to wipe her face.

"My bad." I got up so she could go to the bathroom and clean herself up. For safety measures, I kissed her in the mouth to let her know I didn't feel any different about her and that it was all good. I would still respect her in the morning.

The End

First Day Out: Round One

PATIENCE

Today was one of the happiest days of my life. My man, Stacks, had just come home from doing a bid in the Feds and I couldn't wait to devour his ass. All that sexting and phone sex had finally come to an end. I wanted to feel some real deal ass smacking, hair pulling, and pussy pounding. We talked about it enough over the phone. It was time to see if he could back up all that shit he was talking. I stood in front of him butt-ass naked so he could see my curves and neatly-trimmed peach. He didn't like it bald, said it made him feel like he was fuckin' a baby.

My eyes examined every inch of his chocolate frame until it landed on his thick-ass phallus. This nigga was hung like a horse. My mouth watered in anticipation because I couldn't wait to have that pretty muthafucka in my mouth and down my throat.

Stacks was dark-skinned, 5'9" with a low cut and very little facial hair. He had a little belly from the prison food, but my baby was still sexy. Taking a few steps towards him, I grabbed his wrists one by one and handcuffed him to the bed post. He smiled, waiting on my next move.

"When I told you I was going to suck the skin off yo' dick," I rubbed my nose against his cheek and whispered, "I meant that shit."

Using my finger I traced a line from his chest, stopping at his waist. Squatting on my feet, I stared that python in its one eye before I licked the tip and made it disappear into my mouth until I felt it press against my tonsils. Stacks thrust his hips forward, causing me to gag a little. Pulling back, I cleared my throat and hawked spit on the tip. I liked to give sloppy head. Using both hands, I stroked him hard and put it back in my mouth. My head was moving back and forth at a rabbit's pace.

"Shiiitt." Stacks moaned and threw his head back while I went to work on it.

Pausing for a split second, I looked up at him. His pre-cum was dripping, so I licked it clean.

"Look me in the eyes when I suck yo' dick. That's an order," I demanded.

Stacks dropped his head and smiled at me. "You trying to kill a nigga in this bitch. You know it's been a while for me."

"Nah, you was talking all that shit when you was locked up. I want you to fuck my face just like you promised."

With my eyes still on him, I slid my mouth back on his erection and slurped on it noisily. That shit made my pussy drip juices onto the tile, making a splash like a raindrop. Stacks obeyed my command and rocked his hips hard, giving it to me just like I wanted it. Moisture pierced the back of my eye sockets, and I teared up as he fucked my mouth furiously, killing my throat. At one point in time, I thought I was about to throw up, but I held that shit down.

Stacks started to moan loudly. "I'm 'bout ta nut."

Counting to ten in my head, I pulled his dick out of my mouth, making that popping sound, and jacked his dick. Seconds later, he was busting all over my face and lips, giving me a different type of money shower. Holding my mouth open, I let the rest ooze to the back of my throat. I gargled his babies before I swallowed them all. When I held my head up, I licked the remnants of his cum from my lips and smiled.

Stacks was breathing heavily, but he managed to speak. "I'll kill you if you try and leave me. Yo' ass belong to me."

"Don't worry, my king. I ain't going nowhere and I'll kill you if you give my dick away."

"Un-cuff me so I can beat that pussy up."

His bad boy demeanor turned me on, so I quickly un-cuffed him. It was time for him to give me what was promised.

My pussy had its own heartbeat and she was thumping hard with anticipation. On my way to the opposite side of the bed, I removed my boy shorts and bra, then tossed them on the floor.

"Face down, ass up." He smacked my ass when I slid in front of him.

Crawling on the bed, I stopped when I got to the middle and in the requested position. Stacks eased behind me and tongue kissed my kitty from the back. A strong bolt of electricity shot up my back, causing me to reach for the headboard. His licks were warm as he teased the crack of my ass with his tongue before penetrating my hole. Stacks was the definition of a true freak and I loved that shit. Fucking my ass with his tongue was erotic. My pussy leaked heavily.

Teasing my opening, he rubbed the base against my lips. That was too much for me and I needed to feel him now. Looking back at him, I purred, "Put it in now!"

Stacks obliged and dipped inside me deep. Arching my back, I held my butt cheek while he beat it up. "Mm. Hm."

"Hold that ass open."

Squeezing my cheeks with both hands, he murdered my shit. It almost felt like he was in my chest. Pulling out, he got out of bed and pulled me to the edge. I was still on all fours. Inserting his finger, he moved it in and out slowly. Satisfied, he grabbed the Vaseline from the nightstand and greased my ass.

Slowly he eased his dick in my ass. My eyes stretched in their sockets and I stopped breathing for a few seconds. Anal wasn't my thing, but if he liked it, I loved it. He could fuck me in every hole I had to offer. Starting off slow, he stroked me with ease. That shit didn't help, so I stopped him.

"Wait! I'm not drunk enough."

When he pulled out, I was able to breathe again. Reaching over to the nightstand, I grabbed my cup of Hennessey and downed it. "Okay, I'm ready."

Assuming my position I tooted my ass in the air and prepared myself to take whatever he was dishing. Stacks slipped back in and hit it slow. Once I was comfortable with it, he sped up. Gripping the sheets, I bit down on my lip. "Damn!"

It felt so good, I had to throw it back. This man was beating my ass like he was inside the coochie. However, that was something I should've expected because when he was locked up, he mentioned tearing my ass up when he touched down. Stacks spent that whole round in the back of me. Sticking and moving. We stayed in that position until he nutted all in my ass. Literally. My legs were stiff, so I stretched out across the bed and took a minute to relax.

Stacks wrapped his arm around my waist and held me in his arms. He had my heart and there was no doubt about that. It had been so long since I had a real man in my bed.

"What's on your mind?" He whispered in my ear.

"You."

"What about me?"

"I'm happy you're home. Now we can be happy together. You just don't understand how I feel about you."

"I do. Just be patient and everything will work itself out."

"Oh really?"

"Yes really."

We laid in silence for the next hour. No words were spoken because what was understood didn't need to be explained. Stacks eased his hand on my thigh. His touch alone turned me on. Poking my ass out, I pushed up against him.

Sliding his tongue in my ear, he whispered in my ear, "Open up for me."

The bass in his voice was sexy. At his request, I raised my leg to the ceiling. Stacks slithered inside my wetness and moved slow. Then he pinched my right nipple.

"This pussy good, just like I knew it would be."

"I saved it just for you."

"Fuckin' right. This my shit."

With one hand on my hip, he dove in and out of my slit rapidly. Stacks had my kitty purring and calling his name. Soft moans escaped my lips. The euphoria I felt had me on cloud nine. Turning towards him, I raised my leg higher to gain access to my pearl. Using my fingers, I fondled her aggressively.

"Yeah, play with that pussy for daddy."

My eyes were rolling to the back of my head and my breathing was heavy as hell.

"That dick feel good to you?"

"Yes! Yes!"

Stacks gripped my neck. "Cum on this dick."

My body shivered. "Sss. Ooh. Ah! Ah! Arghhhh!" My insides were crying, as he hit my spot repeatedly. Unable to hold it any longer, a gush of fluids oozed all over him. Stacks didn't stop until he reached his climax. For now, I was tapped out and I needed to be rejuvenated.

THE NEXT DAY

Stacks was in a deep sleep when I woke up the next morning. I knew he was tired because when I slipped from underneath his arm, all he did was roll over and continue to snore. Today was a busy day for me, so I hopped in the shower and washed off last night's scent and fluids. Standing in the mirror, I brushed my teeth and gargled with some mouthwash. A bitch couldn't be walking around with dick on her breath.

Once I was dressed, I went into the kitchen and whipped up a quick breakfast for my man. After the way he put it down last night, he could have breakfast, lunch, dinner, dessert, and snack. I would be the dessert and snack, of course. On the menu was a steak omelet, a side of grits, fruit, and some orange juice. Placing it all on a tray, I walked into the bedroom and set it down on the dresser.

"Baby, get up." I nudged his shoulder.

He mumbled something and rolled over. Determined to get him up, I stuck my hand underneath the blanket and jiggled his balls. "Get up."

His eyes blinked a few times before they were fully open.

"Hmm." He grinned. "You must be ready for another round."

"Not yet. I have a special surprise planned for you so I have to go and get it in order."

"What?"

"Now if I told you, then it wouldn't be a surprise now would it?" I smirked deviously and kissed his lips. "In the meantime, I made you breakfast."

Stacks sat up in bed and looked over at the delicious breakfast I made for him. "I hope that's not swine."

"You know I know better than that."

"Thanks, baby."

"You're welcome. I'll be back, so kick back and relax."

"Don't be gone too long."

"I won't."

Cruising in my BMW, I blasted my music. Kevin Gates's song "Jam" filled my ears. Last night had me in such a good mood. It felt like I had lost ten pounds of water weight. Those multiple orgasms did it for me.

After pulling up to my girl's house, I got out and knocked on the door.

Nyla opened the door. "Hey girl. That nigga let you leave the house?"

"Yep. He has been fucked and fed. Need I say more?" I giggled.

"Yassss, bitch! I know that's right." Nyla closed the door and we went and sat in her living room. "So what's the tea, bitch? Did he put the dick down? I need to know."

"Hell yeah. Don't you see a bitch walking funny and shit?"

"Well, your legs already fucked up so it's hard to say." She always made jokes about my bow legs.

"You just jealous 'cause my shit's sexy."

"I love your legs."

"Sooo…" I hesitated on what I was about to say. "Do you remember what I asked you?"

"What?" Nyla squinted her face like she smelled something foul and rubbed her thighs. She was wearing booty shorts that gripped her thighs like a glove. That bitch was fine too.

"About his gift when he came home."

Nyla was silent for a minute before she blurted out, "The threesome?"

"Yeah."

"No." Nyla rolled her eyes. "I thought you were playing with me."

"I'm dead-ass serious."

"Niggas always want a threesome, but don't have enough dick for one bitch," she snapped.

"Girl, he has dick for days. Thank you."

"Please spare me the details."

Something told me she would be a little salty, but having a threesome was my desire.

"You told me that you would do it. Why the sudden change?"

"I think you know that answer already."

"No, I don't."

"You think I want to see you fuckin' that nigga?"

"Don't act like that." Walking towards her, I straddled her lap and tongue kissed her.

The steamy relationship we had developed over the past few months was nothing I'd ever felt before. Nyla was gentle with the way she handled my body and vajayjay. Sex with her was amazing, but I preferred dick any day. When I decided to wait on Stacks, I promised to never let another man run up in me. Nyla was my substitution. There was no dick involved, only oral play between us.

While caressing my breasts, with one hand, she slipped her free hand underneath my dress. My cat was bouncing with excitement in my panties. Pushing them to the side, she finger fucked me slowly.

"I thought about you all night," she mumbled. "Just thinking about him putting dick in you pissed me off."

"Shhh!" I placed my finger over her lips, then licked them.

Nyla had three fingers in me. Things grew more intense by the second. I rode her fingers the same way I rode her mouth. Leaning closer, I sucked on her neck. Then I rotated back and forth between her nipples with my tongue. Filled completely with pleasure, I released my juices on her fingers. Nyla moved her hand then licked them clean.

"Come to my house at nine and you can suck the pussy too. Stacks is my man and you have to share me."

Nyla thought for a second before she responded, "I'll be there."

"Nine sharp." I kissed her lips. "Don't be late."

"Okay."

ROUND TWO

It was eight o'clock on the dot and we were getting our drink on and smoking a fat-ass blunt. Stacks finally loosened up and turned up with me.

"Where's my surprise?" he questioned.

"Be patient. It's almost that time."

"That shit sound crazy."

"You nervous?"

"Nah. If it's anything crazy, I'm killing you."

Grabbing his hand, I put it between my legs. "This the only thing you gon' kill."

"Facts."

"Come on and let's go take a shower so we can get ready."

"A'ight."

Stacks turned the water on and made it warm. The glass was foggy, but that wasn't the only thing that was hot and steamy. Shit was about to get X-rated in less than an hour. Stepping in, he held my face and kissed me passionately. His tongue moved around in my mouth. Holding it, I sucked on it. My hand made its way down past his belly, which I affectionately called my playground. Grabbing ahold of his balls, I massaged them gently. Pushing him against the wall, I wrapped my hand around the base of his meat and pulled on it, jacking him off slowly, I waited until he was semi-hard before I slid down to my knees. The water spewing from the shower head wet my hair and face.

Closing my eyes, I ran my tongue across the chocolate-covered mushroom-shaped head. Easing it back into my mouth, I devoured him at a slow pace. Stacks massaged my scalp. Moaning, I gripped his balls once more and played with them.

"Suck that dick just like that."

His hips rocked swiftly like a snake moving to my music. He was completely under my control - or so I thought. Stacks gripped my hair a little tighter. His strokes rocked a little harder. Thrusting inside my mouth, he rubbed my face affectionately as he looked into my eyes.

"Damn you look so fuckin' sexy. Swallow that dick."

Placing my hands on his hips, I bobbed fast on his wood.

"Hiccup on that shit."

Locking my jaws, I pulled on it aggressively. Squeezing his meat, I hit the tip and rocked the mic like I was in a rap battle. Many nights I spent time planning how I would please him once I had access to him. Now that I had my man in my possession, we were stuck together forever.

Stacks started to moan loudly. I knew he was about to cum. After pulling out, he stroked it rapidly. Seconds later, he was busting on my face again. The water and semen mixed, so I wiped my face. He helped me to my feet and stuck his tongue in my mouth.

Making our way back to the bed, he laid on his back. "I need a few minutes to re-coop."

That was fine with me since we couldn't get started anyway. While he was stretched out, catching his breath, I was fixing myself a stiff drink. I had been celibate for too long, so I was trying to get painted all night and add a little spice to our relationship. We talked for a few and watched television. By the time I finished my third drink, there was a knock on the door. It was show time.

Nyla walked in wearing a trench coat. "Told you I'll be on time."

"I know you would."

Stacks was laid back on the bed in his boxers when we walked in. Immediately he sat up. "Who is this?"

"Baby, this is my friend Nyla."

Quickly, he pulled back the cover. "I wish you would've said you were having company. I'm damn near naked."

"It's okay. You don't have to cover up. This is your surprise."

"What'chu mean?" His brow creased.

Nyla dropped her coat and his mouth dropped. There was nothing but bare skin showing.

"Don't slobber, baby. You fuckin' both of us tonight," I assured him.

"Huh?" Clearly he was surprised, so I had to show him what I meant.

Nyla and I locked lips and I could see him watching as if he couldn't believe what was happening right before his eyes. Removing my robe, I tossed it to the floor and climbed onto the bed. Nyla put her head between my legs and ate me out.

STACKS

This was some wild shit. Nonetheless, I was enjoying the show. I knew we joked about it over the phone, but I didn't think she was serious about doing it. Nyla was an animal the way she ate the pussy, so I wondered how she ate the dick. Patience was really enjoying it. She was constantly reaching for shit that wasn't there. That made me wonder if it was her first time, but I didn't have to wonder for long. Nyla and Patience switched positions. My girl was munching on the goodies like a pro. Looking in her direction, she signaled me with her finger and pointed it towards her girl. That was the green light to get down and dirty.

I knelt beside her. Nyla turned her head towards me and opened her mouth. Dropping the rod, I filled her jaws to capacity. Like a pro, she slurped me up proper like. Nyla's lips were locked on my shit like vice grips. That made me go a little deeper, making her gag. A nigga was trying to see if she had tonsils or not.

Patience finally pulled her face out of the plate. "Lay down, baby."

She ain't have to tell me twice. Patience straddled my face, while Nyla rode the stick. The twat was warm, wet, and tight. I could feel her muscles clench as she slid up and down on the pole. My toes were dancing their asses off. My brother wasn't gon' believe this shit here.

Patience grinded against my lips, soaking my face. "Suck this pussy, baby. Stick your tongue in it." Her moaning amped me up, so I nibbled on the man in the boat. "Fuuucckk! Just like that. Ooh shit."

While I worked the middle on my baby, Nyla was still working me. As she bounced up and down, I could feel her wetness slide on my skin. "This dick so good," she moaned while playing with my nut sack.

Patience switched positions with Nyla. It was time for her to get some tongue action too. Li'l mama was anxious 'cause she slapped them fat lips right on my mouth. She almost threw her back out trying to grind so hard. Her thighs vibrated hard when I bit down on that pearl.

"Shit! Shit! Fuck! Gawddd damn," she panted. Her juices were mouthwatering, and I slurped everything that dripped.

Patience and Nyla laid on the bed, anxious for the beat down I was about to deliver. "Do her first so I can watch." Patience suggested.

"Say no mo'."

Pushing her legs back, I licked between her flaps and then dove right in. Both of my hands were pressed down against the back of her thighs as I deep stroked her with each glorious inch.

"Deeper."

Putting the pound game down, I went balls deep in the tunnel. I don't know how she managed to move, but shorty was trying to climb the wall.

"Unt. Unt. Don't move. Take all this dick." I put a lock on her legs and knocked the lining out of the cat. Nyla couldn't keep her hands off of me. Shorty kept using her hand to push me away.

"Too deep," she moaned. "Ah! Ah!"

The feeling of my nut rising made me pull out and shake it. If I was nutting in anybody, it was my baby. Patience came close and smirked. "You can't handle all that dick. Move over."

Patience laid on her back and busted it wide open for a nigga. She made it easy for me to slip that tongue in and get it moist. Eagerly, I plunged every inch deep in her tummy and hiked them legs on my shoulders. The hammer was on beast mode. Patience dug her nails deep into my back.

"Punish this pussy, daddy."

Tongue kissing her, I beat it fast until I shot my hot, heavy load in her tummy.

My ass needed a break. Collapsing on the bed, I laid on my back and took a deep breath. A nigga legit needed an oxygen tank in that muthafucka. I was happier than a bitch 'cause these were the best two days out.

The End

AUTHOR CRUSH

DIAMOND

The sound of my notifications ringing constantly pulled me from my beauty sleep. One thing I hated more than anything was to be interrupted, so whoever it was blowing my shit up was about to get cursed clean the fuck out. Snatching my iPhone from my nightstand, I gathered up all the curse words needed to get my point across before I unlocked my screen.

Every thought in my head disappeared when I saw Sosa's name pop up on my screen. His fine ass had me cheesing my ass off. There were five text messages from him, so I opened them with the quickness.

"Damn, I wanna fuck him so bad." I licked my lips thinking of all of the things I wanted to do to him.

Sosa sent me a text message and four full body pictures of him after one of his intense workouts to tighten up his six pack. The man had the body of a Greek god and I was thirsty to lick him up and down and swallow his babies. Maybe even birth a few. My freaky ass would probably drink that nigga's bathwater if he asked me to. Every inch of his body was tatted and that was a turn on in and of itself. I wanted to act out some of those scenes from his books. Just the thought of it made my pussy moist.

See, Sosa was an author. My favorite one, at that. It all started from an inbox, and now we were here. After reading one of his novels for the first time, I fell in love with his writing style and I had to tell him all about it. From there, he would put hearts on all my pics and send me "good morning beautiful" messages. Eventually we exchanged numbers and the context of our conversation went from friendly messages to "I wanna fuck you" messages.

"Shit." After salivating and staring at his caramel frame while rubbing the seat of my boy shorts, I read his text messages.

Sosa: Good morning beautiful. How did you sleep? You

know I have to check on my future wife and make sure she's okay. As you can see I was tightening up your body.

Diamond: Good morning. I slept just fine. Future wife...lol Sosa stop it. It's cute though.

Sosa: I'm being serious. I know you will make a good wife for me. You don't think so?

Diamond: Oh I know for a fact that I would make a good wife. You have to prove that you actually want me like that.

Sosa: Damn you crushed a nigga heart. I thought I was showing you? Come see me so I can change your mind. I get my weekend pass from the halfway house on Friday and I want you here. Everything on me.

Diamond: Hmm...Okay, well I can drive since I'm only three hours away.

Sosa: Cool. I'll send the money to your cash app for a rental and hotel. And make sure the hotel is nice. None of those three star hotels either.

Diamond: I don't do three stars boo. I'm a five star chick.

Sosa: And just know we fucking all weekend and I'm not pulling out. So you may go back home pregnant. I'm only letting you come up for air and to eat.

Diamond: We'll see about that.

Sosa: I guarantee your inner spirit will come out and sit next to you. I don't play and I'm backed up too.

Diamond: That's cute, BUT you have to show me.

Apparently my body felt what I was thinking because my legs started to rock by themselves. He had me horny as fuck. It was funny how he had that effect on me and he had never even touched the box before. While we continued to text, he sent me twenty-five hundred to my cash app. *Shit, he could fuck me in every position for that amount*, I thought to myself. All I could think about was seeing him face to face, so I got on my laptop and booked my rental car. I needed to spend the whole day in Atlanta, so I would get on the road early that morning and pick him up.

Over the next two days I spent time in the mall picking up sexy lingerie for him to see me in. Our first encounter had to be special since we spent so much time capping on the phone about what we would do to each other. I knew what I was bringing to the table. Sosa, on the other hand, I wasn't too sure. His ass spoke a good game, so hopefully he would deliver the way he said he would. If not, he better be prepared to hear my mouth - and not in a good way either.

FRIDAY MORNING
Diamond

Any other week time would've moved at a rabbit's pace. But since I was anxious and excited, time moved at turtle speed. I had been on the road for almost three hours, so it was almost time for the moment of truth. As time winded down, my heart rate increased by the millisecond.

According to my GPS, I was five minutes away and my anxiety was through the roof. A bitch needed a Xanax pill or something to get my nerves in check. The gas station was several feet away from the red light I was sitting at, so I patiently waited for it to change colors. When it was my turn to go, I hit the gas lightly, then made a sharp right turn into the gas station. My eyes lit up as soon as I saw his face. I pulled up and glanced out the window.

Sosa approached the car and opened the door. "Get out and give me a hug, my beautiful wife."

"You always trying to finesse me." Removing my seatbelt, I eased from the car and fell into his muscular, tatted arms.

The scent of his cologne tickled my nose as my face rested in the crook of his neck. He smelled so good that I could eat him alive. Our embrace was tight and long. Sosa thought he was slick when he eased his hands below my waist and squeezed my cheeks. It had been so long that I damn near melted right away.

"Damn. No draws, huh?"

"Easy access."

Sosa backed me up against the car and I could feel his hand go underneath my dress. My eyes closed immediately. It was early, so the gas station was empty. Even if it was full, I wouldn't care. No one knew me. My breathing was a little on the heavy side, anticipating his next move. His fingers brushed across the hood of my pierced vagina, almost causing me to bust a nut. His behavior was so shameless, but I loved it.

"Let me stop," he chuckled, "before I bend you over right here."

"Thank you."

Sosa waited until I was seated to close the door. Then he jogged to the passenger side and got in. I couldn't keep my eyes off of him or his sexy-ass physique, which I had been fantasizing about for months.

"Where to? Are you hungry?"

"Hungry for you." He licked his lips and placed his hand on my thigh.

"I'm serious. What do you want to eat?"

"You. I'm serious about that. If you hungry, we can go eat."

"Nah. I'm good. I ate already. All I want is you."

"Well, let's go to the suite then."

The ride wasn't long or boring because Sosa kept me laughing the entire time. I absolutely loved his sense of humor. That was one of the things that attracted me to him, not to mention the freaky shit he wrote about. He had me curious to see if he was all talk, or if he

44

delivered the D the way he did in his stories. My patience allowed the time to present itself and within the next hour, I would find out. One of two things were about to happen. He was gon' have my ass climbing the walls, or hitting the highway because I wasted my time.

"What you thinking about over there?"

"Nothing," I lied.

"Bullshit. Yo' ass look scared," he teased.

"Nope. I'm not scared of you."

"You scared of this though." From the corner of my eye, I peeped him holding his dick and that shit was thick in his pants. My vaginal juices instantly started to flow. Instantly, one of my legs began to shake out of control.

"Nope. I'm not scared of that either."

"We'll see in the next…" Sosa paused and looked at the GPS mounted on the window. "Five minutes."

Rolling my eyes, I pretended to brush him off. "Yeah, whatever. We'll see about that."

Sosa leaned over and kissed the side of my neck. His tongue soon followed. There went the tingle between my legs once again. "I'm about to slide yo' ass into a coma."

Damn! Me and my cat wanted to scream off of that alone, but I kept it cute. "I hear you."

"Watch yo' inner spirit come out and sit next to you and start talking."

"Boy, bye. Now you just capping." Meanwhile, I was clutching my pearls listening to his freaky ass.

"Nah. No cap, ma. I'm the real deal. I bet I get you pregnant in six hours."

My head swiveled in his direction with a cautionary look on my face. "How? You must have super sperm if you plan on shooting through the condom."

Sosa looked at me like I had five heads. "Hell nah. I'm hitting that raw. You belong to me. I been told you that."

"That's prison talk."

My comment caused him to shift n his seat. For a moment or so he trained his beautiful, scary brown eyes at me and I became weak for a short moment. Finally he spoke, in that sexy country accent.

"Ma, listen to me." He gently grabbed my hand and played with my fingertips. "I meant everything I said and you should know that by now. I've shown you where my interest lies, and that's with you. If I didn't mean it, trust me, you wouldn't be here right now. I'm fucked up about you and I mean that."

Each point he made was valid. However, he knew all about my past and should understand why I was so reserved when it came down to my feelings. Deep down I wanted to hang on to his every word, but then I would be responsible for my own heartbreak and I couldn't have that. My inner crazy would come out and Sosa would be in somebody's Intensive Care Unit for fucking with my feelings. True enough, I was sweet, but once I'm fucked over, I turn into a certified psycho.

"Bae, do you understand me?"

Our destination was fifty feet away, so I remained silent until I found a parking spot. Killing the ignition, I turned to face him.

"I heard everything you've said and been saying, but now you hear me out. Like I told you before, I've been down this road more times that I care to admit, and I'm not interested in being hurt. If you want this to be a fuck thing, then that's cool. I'm grown. I can handle that as long as you're honest about it."

I had to pause and collect the rest of my thoughts because he kept looking at me with those tantalizing eyes. "Seriously, Sosa, don't keep me in the dark about anything. I'll respect you more."

"I ain't gon' lie, I do wanna fuck you."

This nigga nodded his head up and down while grinning at me like something was funny. I wanted to slap the shit out his ass, but I kept my composure because I opened the door on that one.

"But I wanna make love to you forever."

Sosa leaned closer to me and grabbed my face, placing his mouth over mine. Our tongues intertwined and slow danced passionately. The chemistry between us was crazy and I was ready to suck his dick right there in the car. No tints or nothing. It was time to go upstairs, so I broke the kiss expeditiously.

"I'm ready, baby, let's go. You teased me enough."

"I been ready."

After I checked in, we took the elevator to the second floor in search of room 212. I slid the key in, the door unlocked, and I sprinted inside. There was no need to waste time, so I immediately undressed myself and threw my clothes onto the floor. He did the same. The king-sized bed was calling my name, so I crawled to the middle and laid on my back. The nervousness I felt had been replaced with anxiety.

Sosa got up on the bed and pushed my legs apart. Hunger was in his eyes as he took a look at the budding flower between my thighs. The way she was thumping, like a marching bang, sent tingles up my spine, feening for his touch. He leaned forward and came face to face with my kitty and used his tongue as a paintbrush. The way he licked her up, down, and slithered it into my box, amused me. He was so deep I could've sworn I felt him lick my walls. It was obvious he hadn't lost his touch during his prison stint, and I was paying for it.

"Stop!" My lips said one thing, but my body said another. *Bitch, shut up, we love this shit.*

Sosa continued to nibble on my pearl, teasing me, as my juices flowed down my ass crack. Two of his fingers made their way inside, stroking me with the come here motion, summoning my G-spot to erupt. My juices coated his fingers, then he pulled them out slowly. Licking his fingers, he placed them into mine, so we both could enjoy the taste of my sweet nectar.

My body was so anxious to feel him inside of me that I had small shakes. It was our first time, so we were ready to act out the freaky shit we talked about. The rod between his legs was standing tall like the Eiffel tower and it was time for me to feel him deep inside my sacred place.

Sosa leaned down and kiss me gently. Our tongues did a slow dance, creating more friction between us. His pelvis was pressed hard against mine. The tip of his head was pushing anxiously against my lips, paving a way for him to slip inside my slippery slope. The thrust of his rod inside my tight nookie broke my virginity all over again.

"Sss. Mm," I gasped for air.

As he thrust in and out at a steady pace, I clenched my vaginal muscles tight around his stick.

"Fuck yeah!" he grunted. "Grip that dick just like that."

Sosa's voice was just above a whisper as he kissed me again. With our bodies on one accord, I wrapped my legs around his waist. Placing my arms on his shoulders, I pulled his body closer to mine. My man's stroke game grew deeper and the pants that filled his ears were now replaced with moans.

"Ooh. Yes." My stomach clenched every time he pulled out and went back in. My bladder felt full like I had to pee, but I didn't want him to stop. "Go deeper, baby." I begged.

Sosa obliged and delivered, that Grade-A beef, digging deep in my guts. The second he hit that spot, my orgasm made an appearance. The pressure was so intense, I thrust my hips to meet him halfway. My uterine walls started to vibrate. My nails introduced themselves to his back as I dug them deep into his ink covered flesh.

"Sosa, I'm cumming. Shit!" He stepped his game up, placing one leg on your shoulder and pounded the box, knocking the juice out. I felt the warmth creep down my thigh.

"Ah! Ah! I knew you would fuck me good." I bit down on his neck. It felt so good. My insides quaked hard and showered his piece with hot lava.

Sosa continued to put in work until he came inside of me. When he finally released my leg, it felt heavy, yet numb. I couldn't move, so I stayed in that same spot. Lying beside me, he placed his hand on my stomach.

"You alright?"

"Yes, baby. Sore, but I'm good." I giggled.

Just a while ago I was talking big shit to him about how I would have his ass hollering, but he definitely made me out to be a liar.

"Didn't I tell you I was gon' slide yo' ass into a coma?"

"Yep, but I didn't believe you." The smile on my face was wide. I was in love with him and he didn't even know it. The dick was only a bonus.

Sosa kissed my lips. "I just made you a believer."

"Yeah, you did that. I can't lie."

"I'm not finished though." Placing his hand between my legs, he stroked my middle, turning me on. I couldn't keep my hands and lips to myself. Engaging in a slow, passionate kiss, my fingertips ran across his chest and made their way down to his wood. *Damn, he has dick for days,* I thought to myself.

My pussy was wet as fuck. Round two was in full effect. Using his hand to push my legs apart, he climbed between my thighs. Our lips were still locked. Slowly, he dipped inside, putting my legs on his shoulders.

The first deep stroke took my breath away when those inches hit the bottom of my stomach, causing me to break our kiss. That shit hurt like a muthafucka, but I didn't want him to stop either.

"Unh huh. I hit that spot."

No words could leave my lips. Shit, I couldn't breathe either. He was too deep for me. My eyes flickered and fluttered. By now my face was probably flushed from lack of oxygen. Using my elbows, I tried to scoot back.

"I can't breathe."

"Breathe, baby." He smirked. "I can't have you passing out on me."

"Sss. Ooooh shit. I can't, you killing my stomach."

"This what you wanted."

Silencing my moans and screams, he covered my mouth with his and continued to left stroke me to death. He refused to drop my legs. The sound of the headboard knocking and my loud moans made a fresh beat together.

"Say my name."

"Sosa! Sosa!" The sound of his name made a dope remix.

My eyes never left his. I wanted him to see my fuck faces. Sosa lasted ten minutes before he released his warm orgasm inside of me and laid on his back.

"Get on top and ride me."

Control was my thing. I didn't hesitate to straddle his lap so I could ride him in the reverse cowgirl position. As I slid down slowly, his girth filled me completely. With my head leaning, I grabbed his ankles while rocking back and forth to give him a clear shot of him sliding in and out of my wet pussy.

Sosa spread my juices, then penetrated my ass with his finger. My reflexes caused me to grind harder while biting down on my lip. The gushy sound grew louder, as I became wetter by the second.

"Shit! Oh!" Having both holes penetrated at one time was the shit.

"Cum on this dick."

"Mmm. It's coming."

"Let it go."

Sosa fingered me faster and coached me into the most powerful orgasm that I've ever felt. As I glanced over my shoulder, he watched in amusement as my cream glazed his chocolate stick. My inner freak was dying to come out, so I climbed off of him and put my mouth to work. Eagerly, I licked and slurped my leftover juice off of him. Sosa's eyes were bulging as he witnessed me deep throat every inch he had to offer until he tapped out.

VALENTINE'S DAY
Sosa

I watched closely as Diamond stirred in her sleep. A long yawn escaped her lips. The bright light that shone on her face made her lids flutter repeatedly. After struggle blinking for a minute or so, she was finally able to open her eyes completely.

"Good morning, sleeping beauty. Happy Valentine's Day."

"Good morning, handsome, and thank you." A slight smile spread across her soft lips. "How long have you been sitting here looking at me."

"Not long. I just got back from getting us some breakfast, so get up, wash your face, and hit that dragon."

We both shared a laugh. "My breath don't stink."

I leaned down and gave her a pop kiss. "Don't matter. I'll still kiss your sexy ass." Grabbing her hand, I helped her from the bed.

***

After a much needed nap, Diamond woke up to me sliding inside from the back. Planting soft kisses on her neck, I slow stroked her while holding her leg up in the air. As the new owner, I watched in delight as my pussy stuck out like a sore thumb. She was spitting out that tasty cream for me to eat after I was done. Switching positions, I buried my head between her legs to taste her deliciousness. Aggressively, I attacked her kitty to stake my claim. She needed to know that she belonged to me after everything I did for her and to her. Diamond's body shook as she held the top of my head.

"What are you doing to me?" she asked, like she didn't know.

"Writing my name on the inside of this pussy."

I could feel her legs lock down on my head, but I kept sucking on her pearl. "You trying to kill me."

"Cum for me."

"I can't; you sucked her dry."

"I'm not stopping until you bust on my lips and tongue."

Forcefully, I used both hands to pin her legs down, going back to attack mode. Diamond moaned, bucked, and tried to wiggle away from me, but that wasn't happening. I spent too much time on lock, dreaming about the day I would be able to suck the life out of some pussy. And over the past few months, I decided that she would be the one I gave my tongue, dick, and heart to. She was solid and kept a nigga in a positive space during the end of my journey.

Her body finally gave in and dripped that nut on my tongue. Satisfied, I released my strong grip and set her free.

Lying on my back, I slapped Diamond on the thigh. "Get on top and ride it. I want ya toes up, ass down."

My dude was limp, so Diamond got on her knees and faced the opposite direction. Her ass was damn near in my face, but I enjoyed the view. She stroked it a few times before I felt her mouth wrap around the tip. Leaning over, I fucked her with my fingers until she dripped, while she spit and choked on me. Once he was standing tall, she saddled up and eased down on it until my dude disappeared into her tight walls.

Diamond had my knees buckling when she came up to the top and slid back down. The feeling of me caressing the inside of her gushy kitty was euphoric.

"Speed it up," I demanded, while gripping her ass and spreading her cheeks, so her cum can rush down my dick.

Playing in her juices, I greased her ass and stuck my thumb inside, making her buck harder like she was riding a bull. "Ah! Baby! Baby!"

"Yeah. Ride that dick, baby." I fingered her faster. "Bounce on daddy's dick." Diamond followed every instruction I gave her.

Switching positions, I stood on the side of the bed and stroked my piece. "Bring that ass to me. Toot it up."

Diamond turned around and shook her booty in the air before backing up to me while I waited like a hungry hyena. Giving her asshole a wet kiss and lick, I rubbed my erection up and down her slit and ass while enjoying the sight of all that chocolate. Finally, sticking it in her slippery pussy, I fingered her booty while she arched up higher in the air.

"Spread that ass some more." I began to slow stroke, listening to it speak back while I hit that spot. Diamond let out a few screams while gripping the sheets, so I pulled out and planted kisses on her back.

"I love you, Diamond. Tell daddy how good I make that pussy feel!"

"So good, baby. Put it back in me," she moaned, displaying a freaky fuck face. "I love you, daddy," Diamond whined, looking back over her shoulder at that dick pumping deep in them guts.

With both hands on her shoulders, I went hard. "You gon' have my baby?"

"Yes."

"You sure?"

"Yes."

"Where you want me to nut at? In that pussy?"

"Ooh. Yes."

"Tell me," I demanded.

"Nut in this pussy, baby." Diamond threw it back, and my thrusts matched hers.

After drilling her hard and pulling her hair, I nutted deep into her treasure box.

As she laid peacefully in my arms, I couldn't help but to stare. I loved everything about her and I couldn't risk not seeing her again. Before she left the ATL, we were going to make arrangements to get her relocated. I closed my eyes and drifted off into a deep sleep.

The End

FOR THE LOVE OF A THUG

JANAE

This nigga had been on my radar ever since I pulled up at my daddy's trap spot. He was a nice honey dip and he was definitely feeling me. I could tell by the way he was checking me out. My mother had just passed away and I was having a mental meltdown. That day flashed through my mind like yesterday.

I stepped onto the porch and hugged my dad tight. "Hey baby. It's gon' be okay. I'm here for you."

"Shidd, me too," Skeet added.

"Nigga, my niece don't need you," Coop spoke up.

"Niece?" Skeet questioned.

Letting him go, I wiped my eyes with the back of my hand. Brick, my father, then turned towards Skeet. "Yeah, this my daughter. So keep yo' eyes off of this one."

"Ohhh shit! My bad, big dawg."

Coop stepped in and hugged me as well. "We got'chu, baby. Whatever you need, just let me know."

"Let's go. Get up with me as soon as you hear something." He dapped Skeet up, then we left.

There was something about him that had me intrigued besides his dreads and tattoos. Seeing him would certainly be a problem for Brick, so I knew I would have to be careful. We locked eyes the moment I saw him, but I looked away so as not to make it so obvious. I already knew that we would bump heads eventually, so I had to be patient.

Me and the girls headed out to the club on a Saturday night and ended up in an after hour spot in Pompano. We were tipsy as hell. As I slid through the crowd, I had my hand over my cup. Brick always told me to watch my drink when I went out. Safety was mandatory in his book.

"Girl, it's some fine niggas in here tonight!" Kim shouted. We posted up near the dance floor and got our party on.

The DJ was blasting Quavo's new jam, "Workin' Me." The ratchet stage hit me quick. Tongue out and ass up, I was shaking this ass like it was going out of style.

Attempting to talk over the music, I shouted, "This my shit!" Kim and Tay were dancing with me.

We were approached by three dudes dressed like the group Rae Sremmurd. Yeah, I definitely wasn't impressed. The one with the brush cut was skinning and grinning. "What's up, sexy ladies?"

"Nothing. What's up with y'all?"

"Shit. We looking for some babies to slide with."

"Well goo goo gaga shit." Kim was drunk as hell. All I could do was shake my head.

"Where y'all going?" Tay asked.

Their spokesperson was grinning and licking his lips like he was ready to slide up in something. "Shit, we got a suite on the beach. What y'all wanna do?"

"Shit, we tryna slide too."

Kim was pissing me off being so thirsty and whorish. "I'm going to the bathroom. I'll be back."

One of his friends grabbed my hand. "You need help, ma?"

Snatching away from him, I replied, "I've been wiping this pussy by myself for eighteen years, I can manage."

Highly irritated, I stormed off in search of nothing in particular. As I headed to the back, I spotted a familiar face. Obviously he spotted me too since he started smiling. Of course I had to play hard to get.

"Wassup, sexy?"

Skeet grabbed my arm, but I pulled away quickly, pretending to have a major attitude. When he shook his head and laughed, I looked him up and down. A smile appeared across my lips. Stepping closer to him, I licked my lips. No one was around to stop my show.

"Nothing much. What's up with you?"

Checking out the merchandise, his eyes wandered all over my body. That was when he decided to shoot his shot. "Shit. What you 'bout to get into?"

"Janae!" A female screamed my name before I could answer him. I already knew who it was coming to cock block. "Girl, I been looking for you."

"What?" She didn't need to be nowhere near me talking shit.

"We about to slide with these dudes, so come on," Kim blurted out in front of Skeet.

"No. I told you I'm not going. We don't know them."

She folded her arms across her chest.

When we started fussing, he intervened. "You Brick's daughter, Janae, right?"

Playing it off, I rolled my neck in his direction. "Um. Yeah. How do you know my daddy?"

"I work for him. That day you came to the shop, I was there."

"Oh, I do remember seeing you there."

Kim caught an attitude. "Girl, what you gon' do?"

"I'll take you home. It's not a problem," Skeet spoke up.

"Umm. You sure about that?" I had to double check because I wasn't sliding with them hoes.

"Yeah. I'll make sure you get home safe. I know how Brick is and I don't want no problems from him about you."

"Go ahead, Kim. I'm going home. Be safe."

Kim giggled. "I promise I'll use a condom." Then she walked away in a hurry, ready to be fucked.

"You need to find you some better friends," he grilled.

Seductively, I played with the charm on his Cuban link. My ass was definitely tipsy and horny. "Well, maybe you can be my new friend."

Ignoring my comment, he placed his hand on my waist. "Come on, let's get out of here."

His friend was leaning and out of his mind, so Skeet tapped him on the shoulder. "Aye bro, let's ride."

Bopping through the crowd, I was too lit. I could barely walk a straight line. Wrapping his arm around my waist, Skeet escorted me out the door and through the parking lot. After opening the car door, he helped me into the front seat. Skeet leaned in towards my face and for a second, I thought he was about to kiss me. The back door opened and his drunk-ass homeboy fell headfirst into the backseat. Dude took wasted to another level. He definitely ruined our moment. Closing both doors, Skeet stepped over to the driver's seat and got in.

Skeet started the engine and put the A/C on max. The air felt good blowing against my hot body. Bending forward, I took off my heels. My feet were burning.

"You good, ma?" he asked.

"Yeah, I'm good. I just had to take these shoes off."

"Just making sure. Where do you live?"

"In Melrose. I'll show you just drive."

"Got it, boss lady."

Thirty minutes later, we were pulling up in my driveway. Skeet put the truck in park and looked over in my direction.

"You live here alone?"

"Yeah, now I do." The thought of being without my mother was fucking with me badly. Liquor and grief was a painful combination. That caused me to exhale deeply. "I was living here with my mom, but she passed away a little over a week ago. So, it's just me now."

His demeanor changed quickly. "Damn, ma. I'm sorry to hear that."

Shifting in my seat, I grew silent. Tears started to run down my cheeks. Grabbing my hand, he caressed it a little. "I apologize for bringing that up. Are you going to be okay?"

Shaking my head, I replied. "No. I haven't slept here since she passed away." That was the truth. Since she died, I had been staying at Demarcus's house with him and his mom.

"Come on. I'll walk you in." He was a complete gentleman. Skeet stepped around and opened the door, then escorted me to the front door.

The inside of the house was dark and the only lighting available was coming from the street lights. In a drunken stumble, I moved around the house as if I was a stranger in my own home.

"You good?"

"Yeah. I found the switch." No sooner had I said that than the light lit up the living room.

"Well, I just wanted to make sure you got in okay. I'm about to head out."

"Can you stay for a little bit please?" Little did he know, he was staying because my puppy dog eyes had the charm to win anybody over. I'd been doing that to Brick for as long as I could remember.

Skeet walked over to the sofa and sat down. "Sure."

"Thank you." Coming off as if I was shy, I sat down beside him and looked in the opposite direction. There was a lot on my mind and I truly wanted someone to talk to.

"What's going on? You can talk to me," he suggested with sincerity.

At first I remained silent, but then I turned in his direction and put my legs up on the sofa. "My life will never be the same now that my mom is gone. She was supposed to be the one dropping me off at college in the fall and now she's not here. She won't see me graduate, have kids, or get married. Life is not fair."

"I understand your pain, but at least you still have your dad. He can't take your old girl's place, but at least you're not alone."

"I know, but things are just complicated with him right now. We had a blow up the other day and I haven't spoken to him yet."

Skeet moved closer to me and played with the strands of my hair. "Whatever it is, y'all can get through it together. Life is too short to hold grudges against the ones you love. Let that go and have a conversation with him."

"Honestly…" I wiped my eyes and sighed heavily. "I don't know what to think. It's not him that has the problem. It's his girlfriend, baby mama, or whoever the fuck she is. She don't like me."

"Why wouldn't she like you? And I don't see Brick allowing a woman to interfere with his relationship with his daughter. I just don't see that."

"That's because we just found out he's my dad. My mom didn't tell us until she was on her dying bed. All my life I was raised thinking he was my God daddy, but now things have changed."

"Damn! That's a lot to take in, but at the end of the day, he's still your dad. When you get up in the next few hours, call him."

"Okay," I agreed.

Destiny Skai

Skeet looked at his watch like he had somewhere to be. That was when it dawned on me that he might have a girlfriend. Hopefully that wasn't the case. "Listen, ma, I would love to sit and chat with you, but I have to get this drunk-ass nigga home. I'm going to give you my number in case you need to talk."

"Thanks. I appreciate that." He locked his number in my phone.

"Call me anytime and I'll be here to listen to you vent and give you advice."

It hurt that he had to leave me, but to thank him, I leaned forward and wrapped my arms around his neck. My grip was tight. I wanted him to know that I didn't want to let go. Finally, I pulled back just a little and gazed into his eyes. That was my chance to make my move. It felt weird being the aggressor. That was something I never did before. Demarcus was my first everything. Closing my eyes, I moved close to his face and kissed him on the lips. He didn't fight it, so that was confirmation in my eyes to keep going. Easing onto his lap, I straddled him. Skeet's hands caressed my ass while he pushed up my dress.

"Don't leave yet," I whispered while holding his face close to mine. Using my free hand, I slid his zipper open and touched his thick pecan tan wood. He became hard as soon as I touched it. Boldly, I confessed, "I wanna have sex with you."

It was now or never, so I stopped our kiss and stood in front of him. He focused hard and closely as I removed my dress and thong. Skeet had pure seduction written all over his face. Unbuckling his pants, he slid them down along with his boxers. Once again I mounted his lap and kissed hard and with aggression. The liquid courage was in full effect. Slowly, I eased down on him. He was packing more than my boyfriend and it hurt going up in me. My tight, inexperienced pussy had his dick in a chokehold and I was doing my best not to scream.

"Fuck!"

He smacked me on the ass as I started to grind on him halfway and in a circular motion. Skeet's hands were on both cheeks, pushing me all the way down on him. He made sure every inch was stuffed inside.

"Ouuuu! Ow. Shit."

To suppress the noise, I buried my face on the side of his neck and sank my nails into his shoulders. As I rode him long and hard with his assistance, I was finally into it. That pain turned into pleasure. Skeet placed his hand around my throat and squeezed it. Nice and fast, he pushed hard against my middle and had me moaning like crazy. His eyes fluttered and he bit his lip. That was a face I recognized.

"Fuck! I'm cumming," he grunted.

After we were done, I got up and left the room and returned with a washcloth. Taking it from my hand, he wiped himself off and got dressed. We stood face to face and kissed once more.

"I hope this won't be the last time I see you."

"Nah, it won't be," he assured me and walked out the door.

The sun was coming up when I was going to bed. As I laid there staring at the ceiling, I smiled. "That's what thug love feel like, huh." My boyfriend never made me feel like that.

Rolling over on my side, I tucked my body pillow between my legs and held it tight. I didn't know what was about to happen next, but I sure as hell couldn't wait to find out.

***

SKEET

Janae called and texted me later on that day, but I couldn't answer the phone since I was in the hospital with Kamari. Shit got real crazy when I left her house. I ran down on that nigga Raheem and his crew. There was a shootout and my nigga got clapped up. I knew she thought a nigga did a dash and go, so I had plans to hit her up later and let her know what was up.

As I pulled up in the parking lot of my complex, I got out of the truck and reexamined it. There were several bullet holes in it, so it was mandatory that I got that fixed. After unlocking my door, I stepped inside and pushed the door closed. It immediately flew back open. Reaching for my weapon, I upped the fie and stupid-ass Jenn walked in with a frown on her face.

"You gon' shoot me now?"

"What the fuck you doing here?" I set the gun on the television stand.

"Why haven't you called me yet?"

"As you can see, I'm just getting home."

Now wasn't the time for Jenn and her bullshit, so I left her standing there and went to my bedroom. Her ass was hot on my trail and still talking shit.

"So where you been all day? And who is the bitch?" She flopped down on the bed and crossed her arms.

"I don't know what you talking about." Steadily ignoring her, I removed my shirt and tank top, exposing my many tats.

Jenn was focused on a nigga hard as I removed the rest of my clothes. When I was down to my boxers, she walked over and stood in front of me.

"You said you were coming home to rest. You lied."

Highly annoyed, I rolled my neck. "Man, go on with all that."

Jenn grabbed my face. "What the fuck is this?" She pushed my dreads out of the way.

"What?"

"All these marks?"

"I don't - "

Before I could utter another word, she slapped me in the face. My reflexes kicked in and I grabbed her by the throat and pushed her against the wall. "Don't put yo' fuckin' hands on me. I done told you that already."

"Fuck you!" she spat. "I'm just supposed to sit around while you out fuckin' different hoes?"

"Bitch, I been in the hospital all morning with Kamari." When I let her go, I mushed her in the face. "Stupid-ass girl."

"Yeah, whatever."

"Bruh, go home. I'm not in the mood for this shit."

"You just wait. I got something for you," she threatened as she walked out.

62

Jenn didn't know I was glad she left with her aggy ass. That gave me time to shower and get dressed. After slipping on a pair of Champion sweats, tee, and matching sneakers, I put on my Cuban link and bracelet. My cologne of choice was Versace. On my way out the door, I hit up Janae.

"Yeah," she answered dryly.

"Damn, ma, why you sound like that? You good?"

"Yep."

"You must be mad at me?"

"Nope."

"Damn, why all the one word answers?"

"No reason," she stated slickly.

"You home? I'm about to slide up on you."

"Yeah."

"A'ight. I'm on my way."

Janae hung up the phone fast as hell. I knew she was mad, but all of that was about to change in the next twenty minutes.

When I arrived I knocked on the door. Janae opened the door and she had a mean unit on her face. It was cute, so I laughed it off.

"Stop looking so mean." I leaned forward and kissed her soft, pink-ass lips. "I know you mad 'cause I been ignoring your calls and texts, but I had an emergency."

"I hear you." She rocked on her heels.

"Come here. Let me show you something." Janae followed me to my truck.

"What?"

"You see them bullet holes?" She nodded her head. "These niggas was shooting at me after I left here and my homeboy got shot. I been at the hospital with him all day."

The frown on her face slowly disappeared. "I'm sorry to hear that. Is he going to be okay?"

"Yeah, he gon' pull through." I held her waist. "I know what you was thinking and for the record, I'm not a slime ball-ass nigga. I wasn't gon' do you like that."

"I know. My bad." She smiled.

"There goes that smile I like." Pulling her close to me, I kissed her again. But that time I added some tongue with it. She pulled back and wiped her lips with her finger.

"Go get dressed so I can take you to dinner or something."

"I don't feel like sitting in at a restaurant, so can we just grab it to go."

"Whatever you wanna do is fine with me."

While Janae showered and got dressed, I sat on the sofa and waited patiently. Jenn was sending me all these crazy-ass messages, but I ignored every last one of them.

We ended up at this spot in Lauderdale Lakes called Chef Pats. The food was banging. No doubt about that. We ordered two crab trays to go and went back to her spot.

"Brick not gon' pop up on us, is he?" The last thing I needed was him sliding up on me while I was sliding up in his daughter. He was my big brother and mentor, but I couldn't stop fuckin' with his daughter. I was digging her too much.

"No," she giggled. "Why, you nervous?"

"Hell yeah. That's my nigga, and I know how he feels about his baby."

"So why you here then?"

"Cause I fuck wit'chu the long way. You worth the consequences."

Janae pressed her lips together. "Hmm. I see." She unlocked the door and we disappeared behind it. "Well, I feel the same way."

She turned on the television in her room and put on *Queen of the South*. "What you know about that?" I asked.

"I love this show."

"You trying to be like your daddy, huh?"

Janae laughed, while sucking on a crab leg. "No. I just like it."

My mind was on sex as I watched her eat. It made me wonder what that mouth do. "I bet you do."

We were one episode in and done with our food. I was ready to go to the next step and apparently, so was she.

Janae stood up and removed her clothes, leaving on her under garments. Sliding back into bed, she covered her body with the blanket. Inching towards her, I positioned myself on top of her and covered my lips with hers. My hands were on the prowl until they made their way to the center. Rubbing her gently, I pushed her panties to the side and rubbed the clit. Her breathing changed and I could feel her humping against my hand. That thang was wet-wet.

Pulling the cover back, I removed her black silk panties and tossed them to the floor. Passionately, I planted soft kisses on her stomach, all the way down to her thighs. Face to face with the kitty, I gave it a few strokes of my warm tongue before I dipped it inside. My whole head was in it. I wanted her to feel me lick her ovaries. Leaving no stone unturned, I nibbled on her clit and she lost it.

"Ah! Shit. Ah! Shit." Her legs clamped down on my head, so I used my hands to hold them open.

"Cum on my tongue," I demanded.

Inserting two fingers, I poked her over and over while licking and sucking. It took her a while to cum for me, but when she did, that muthafucka was like a heavy rainfall.

Satisfied with the outcome, I got up and got naked. Janae opened up for me with no hesitation as she anticipated feeling me inside of her. Taking my time, I put the stick against her plump lips and pushed past her flaps. Wetness was all I felt as I eased down her slippery slope. Her body tensed up from my touch.

"Gawd!" Janae moaned and wrapped her legs around my waist giving me full access to her most sacred treasure.

Slowly, I dipped in and out. I couldn't risk nutting too fast. With each stroke, I went deeper and faster. Soon the sound of the headboard was on one accord with every stroke.

"Ahhhhh," she moaned. "It feels so good."

Janae was still a rookie, but not me. I been fucking since I was thirteen. Therefore, I was familiar with the female body. Especially once I experienced some bomb-ass sex from an older chick. She taught me everything I needed to know about pleasing a woman and how to give it to her.

Applying my weight down on her, I placed both hands on the top of her head, giving her no chance to wiggle at all. As expected, Janae had those claws she called nails in my back. "Throw it back for me."

Janae moved her hips with me, while holding on to my waist. "Oh God!" she hissed. "Why you doing me like this?"

"You like it? It feel good to you?" I breathed heavily in her ear.

"Yesss!" Janae's tongue rolled around my neck, and that was a turn on for me.

Her question told me she was gon' be fucked up after I put this dick on her. See, earlier, I didn't put in any work. That was all her. All I did was guide her pace. Li'l mama was about to be dick crazy, just like Jenn. But I had to keep a handle on that. If things got crazy between us and she went crying to her daddy, there would be a huge problem between us. I couldn't let that happen.

Janae loosened her grip around my waist when she felt me move. I grabbed one of her legs and placed it on my shoulder and straddled the other. Squeezing her butt cheek, I plunged in fast and sank deep.

"Shiiitt!" She clutched her pillow and buried her face in it.

It was truly a pleasant sight to see her fold and moan under pressure. Her titties jiggled every time I slammed against her ass. Taking one in my hand, I squeezed it like a stress ball. The tip of my head hit the bottom as I continued to beat her back in.

"Don't hide. Let me see that fuck face." Moving the pillow away, I tossed it on the floor. Janae didn't look me in my eyes. Instead she turned her head like I couldn't see her cute ass. Her moans were on repeat while she choked the life out her sheets.

Sweat protruded from my forehead, but I ignored it. The deeper I went, the louder she got. That was music to my ears. A buildup of pleasurable pressure that I had been working towards finally showed up. The tingling sensation in my sack was almost too much to bear. The intensity was so severe that it felt like bolts of lightning shooting through my body.

It felt like my dick was having contractions as a gush of semen came spilling out heavily into her womb. Tired wasn't the word for what I felt at that moment, so I crashed onto the bed beside her all out of breath and shit. Janae faced me and rested her leg on me.

"You good?"

"I'm better than good." She ran her hand across my chest.

"You trying to stroke my ego?" My sex game was awesome, so that wasn't a real question.

"Nooo!" That response was long-winded and sounded incomplete.

"Why you say it like that?"

"This is so embarrassing." She paused.

"What?" Now she had me curious.

"I've never had head before or an orgasm."

She had to be fuckin' with me. "Stop playing."

"I'm so serious. I've never had sex that good before."

"Ohhh shit! I done fucked up now."

"Yep! You did." Janae giggled and rested her head on my chest.

JANAE

Lord have mercy! That man fucked my entire soul out of my body. I didn't know where our situation was going, but I knew I wanted more. My father Brick was going to be a problem though. He made it very clear for Skeet to stay away from me and we both ignored that order. But hey, I liked what I liked. I wasn't worried about Demarcus because I would break up with him. The only thing left to do was find out if he had a girlfriend or not. Although that should've been something I established before I let him have sex with me raw and nut in me like we were a couple.

A few hours had past and Skeet was lying there with his eyes closed, but I knew he wasn't asleep. "I should've been asked you this…" His eyes popped open. "Do you have a girlfriend?"

In my heart, I desperately wanted him to say no. If he had one, I was gon' be pissed the fuck off. That's something I would've expected him to tell me. True enough, I had a dude, but we weren't seeing eye to eye lately.

"I'm not gon' lie to you. There was this girl I was dealing with, but I don't fuck with her like that no more."

"Not like that?" I questioned with a frown. "What does that mean? You still messing around with her here and there?"

"It means that she's nothing to worry about. I'm where I want to be: here with you trying to see where this is headed. You see it's late and I'm still here."

"Oh, I'm definitely not worried about her. I'm just curious."

"Don't be. I keep it a bill at all times. I'm single."

"Well, since you keep it a hundred, are you still having sex with her?"

"I haven't."

"When was the last time?"

"I don't remember."

"Yeah, okay."

"Fuck her. I don't wanna talk about that."

"What do you want to talk about?"

"I don't wanna talk." Skeet rubbed my lips with his hand. "I wanna see what these lips feel like."

"You already know what they feel like."

"No, I don't." Skeet was smirking when he closed his eyes briefly. His arm started moving and when I looked down, he was jacking off. I wasn't slow, so I knew what he was talking about.

"I don't suck dick."

"What's wrong with that?"

"Nothing, I guess. I never did it before."

Skeet lifted his head up a little bit. "What kind of lame-ass nigga you been messing with?"

"I don't know."

"That's crazy. I'll show you if you willing to learn."

I thought about it for a minute or so before I replied. "Okay." Demarcus and I had both been virgins, so there were a lot of things we didn't do. All this shit was foreign to me.

Skeet sat up and put his back against the headboard. "Face me and get on your knees," he instructed.

Nervousness took over my body, but something told me that if I wanted him, this was what I had to do. On my knees, I faced him with my hands in my lap.

"Put your mouth on it and move your head up and down. Don't use your teeth though."

Going down, I wrapped my lips around it and did what he said. Skeet put his hand on my head. "I'm going to guide your pace."

Moving my head up and down, I sucked him slowly. I've had the pleasure of watching some porn videos so I knew the concept of it. I just didn't think I would do a good job with it.

"Act like you sucking on a lollipop."

Skeet walked me through it for a few before I caught on. I could taste the pre-cum, but I didn't say anything. Kim was always telling me stories about how she sucked dick and swallowed the nut. She claimed that was why niggas were crazy about her and that's what I wanted with Skeet. I needed this nigga to be hooked on phonics when it came to me.

On this one video this girl spit on the tip, but that was too advanced for me. Next time I did this, I would be better prepared to do some extra shit. In the meantime, I focused on strictly sucking and keeping my teeth out of the way.

"Just like that. Keep them lips on that dick, baby."

Skeet's moans sounded euphoric and it made me feel like I was doing it right. Closing my eyes, I tried not to think about it as much. His hand was running all over my scalp while he continued to push my head down.

"Fuckin' right. Grab my nuts."

I did everything he was telling me to do.

Honestly, I was enjoying doing it. He didn't have a problem eating me out, so I didn't mind returning the favor. Skeet's leg started to tremble. "Shit! I'm about to bust. Don't stop."

I figured that was a good thing, so I kept going. His grip on my hair was tighter than before. His dick stabbed me in the back of the throat and choked me. It felt like I was about to throw up when I gagged. My movement stopped.

"Keep going," he demanded while steadily forcing my head down. "It's coming. Shit!"

My eyes were burning.

"When I buss, swallow it."

Warm fluid shot to the roof of my mouth and I coughed violently. His semen covered his limp dick. Moving his hand, he took a deep breath. "Damn! You did good."

I could taste his semen on my tongue, so I licked my lips and swallowed. It took me by surprise when he tried to kiss me. Curving him, I moved my head to the side.

"Let me brush my teeth first."

"For what? That's my shit and it's clean."

I didn't think he would kiss me after his dick was in my mouth. Skeet tongued me down, then flipped me on my stomach. He spread my cheeks and I felt his tongue tickle my booty hole. I damn near lost my mind. He licked and sucked my pussy from the back before he hit fucked me doggy style. The whole time he dug in me from the back I whined and moaned my ass off. It felt like he was literally in my stomach and rearranging my organs.

By the time he was finished with me, I could barely walk to the bathroom. My lips were swollen and when I peed, that shit hurt. If he thought I was leaving him alone after he did all that freaky shit to me, he had another thing coming. *Bitch, we together now!* All I had to do now was break off things with Demarcus and figure out a way to tell my daddy. There was no way in hell I was leaving this nigga for nobody. Brick was gon' have to accept that I'd do anything for the love of a thug.

The End

Thug Luvin'

SKAI

Look at this lame-ass nigga down on his knees crying. If he thinks I'm taking him back, he got another thing coming. I rolled my eyes and batted my lashes to stir up some tears as I waited for his show to be over.

"Skai, I'm sorry for lying to you. Please don't leave me. I love you."

"Lucci, I can never forgive you for what you did to me. You've constantly lied and cheated on me for years and you think I'm supposed to ignore the fact that you got me looking like a dumb-ass bitch? Nah, I don't think so."

"I didn't know how to tell you," he sobbed.

"Well, you should've found a way. Your lying-ass family members knew what was up and they didn't tell me shit. Fuck all y'all, on God."

"My family loves you, Skai."

"Fuck your family. That includes your phony-ass mammy and sister."

"Skai, please!" he begged. "Don't do this to us."

"You did this to us. Now get out and take your shit with you."

"Not until we finish talking."

"Leave now before I say something I won't regret."

"Just give me another chance, please."

"Get out, Lucci, IT'S OVER!"

Lucci and I had been together for six years. We had plans on getting married and starting a family. However, that plan came to an end when a reliable source exposed his secret.

He continued to beg and plead, but once he realized I wasn't changing my mind, he got up and headed to the door. Lucci looked back one last time with tears in his red eyes.

"I love you, Skai, and I'm sorry." And just like that, he was gone.

After all we'd been through, I couldn't believe that he would betray me in the worst way humanly possible. There was no forgiving him and no second chances. The only thing on my mind was payback and some bomb-ass dick. I needed to release this built up stress. Grabbing my phone, I hit up my go to nigga.

"What's up, baby girl?" Meech answered, sounding spicy.

"I need a fix."

"Come through. I'm at the house."

"I'm on my way."

When I sat down in my Lexus coupe, I put my shades on and backed out of the parking lot jamming "Fuck Boy" by Trina. On my way to Meech's house, I stopped by the liquor store and grabbed a bottle of Patron and some wrap. There were a few dudes standing outside whistling at me as I walked back to my car. I knew I was giving those niggas life in my fitted jeans that gripped my ass so tight and my crop top.

"Aye, li'l mama, bring that ass here."

Rudely, I stuck up my middle finger. "Go fuck ya mama, nigga."

"What you said, bitch?" one of them shouted.

They weren't worth my time or energy, so I got into my car and sped off. Meech lived right by the liquor store, so it took me all of three minutes to pull up and knock on the door. He opened the door with a smile, shirtless. He had the abs of a Greek god, a body he worked for during his incarceration.

"What's up, baby?" He met me halfway and gave me a pop kiss on the lips.

I scurried inside and he closed the door behind me. "I bought us some Patron so we can have a celebratory drink."

"What are we celebrating?" He seemed a little confused.

"Me and Lucci are over. It's finally over."

I fixed two drinks, passed one to Meech, and set the bottle on the table in the living room. We both downed them and I fixed us another round quickly. We did the same thing again.

My body was hot and I needed to be cooled off. Unbuckling my pants, I eased them down to the floor and stepped out of them. Placing one hand on the arm of the chair, I used the other hand to slap my own ass. That shit sounded like thunder. "Come kill this pussy, baby."

Meech walked up behind me and stepped out of his shorts and boxers. "Oh I'm 'bout to."

Grabbing my hair, he pulled my head back and kissed me in the mouth. My pussy was throbbing badly, as he rubbed the tip of his dick up and down my throbbing lips.

"Just put it in," I begged.

"I got this, so be quiet."

His voice was stern and made me wetter. I loved how he always took control. My juices were running down my leg, but he was still teasing me. "Baby, fuck me, please," I begged.

"You want this dick bad, huh?"

"Yesss!" I purred. "Now give it to me."

"I want you to beg for this dick," he teased.

"Please give me the dick, baby. I need it."

"Say my name when you beg."

"Meech, please give me the dick, baby. I'm begging you. You got my pussy so wet right now." Twirling my ass, I attempted to tease him, but he wasn't giving in just yet. The sound of him smacking his dick against my wet pussy was turning me on bad and I was ready for him to beat me down.

"A'ight, I'ma give it to you."

Meech pushed me down further against the sofa and shoved his dick in me. Not gently either.

"Ooh yes, baby, just like that."

"Unh huh," he grunted.

Meech finally let go of my hair, gripped my cheeks, and pounded my ass hard as fuck. All I could do was moan and bite down on my lip. He was very blessed with the stick and he knew how to use that muthafucka. The dick was all in my stomach. I could've swore I felt my kidney slide to the left.

"Beat this pussy, daddy."

"Spread them cheeks for me."

My chest was flat on the leather chair. Reaching back, I put my hand on my ass and opened it up for him. He drilled me with no remorse. My body rocked hard and so did my head.

At any moment, it felt like my neck was going to break. His thrusts were fierce and it felt so good going in and out my pussy. A nice hard fuck was exactly what I needed to take my mind off of the crazy shit that had happened earlier.

Meech fucked me in that same position for at least twenty minutes. Every time he was about to cum, he would stop and slap his dick against my ass to make it last longer. After a few more pumps and a couple of groans, I could feel his body shake. Then he was busting all over my ass.

"Damn, Skai, you got some good-ass pussy."

"The better to tame you with, my dear." I looked over my shoulder and smiled.

"Is that right?"

"Issa fact."

Meech helped me up from the couch and I headed towards the bathroom with a huge smile on my face. Once inside, I closed the door and stood in front of the mirror.

"You a bad bitch, Skai. Now it's time to really fuck some shit up." I blew a kiss to myself in the mirror before I hopped into the shower.

***

Meech

Later on that evening, I took Skai out for a night on the town. Dinner cruises were her favorite thing to do. The first time I took her, she really enjoyed herself. After everything she had been through, I wanted her to have fun and focus on what was in front of her: me.

The day I met Skai was the day I knew that I would do anything to get her. I knew about her punk-ass nigga, but I didn't give a fuck about his bitch ass. We weren't tight like that, so me snatching his girl from underneath his nose didn't faze me one bit. She was all friendly and shit, so I knew she was feeling me. Lucci was out doing his dirt, so when she called me crying, I invited her to my spot to talk. After a few drinks and a blunt, I was digging in them guts. From that point on, we started creeping on the regular. Skai told me she was tired of him and wanted to be with me. In life, you have to appreciate what you have before it shows you what you lost. Lucci waited until it was too late to get some act right about himself. He slipped up and I lucked up.

Skai was dressed in a black sheer dress with a high split up the thigh that I bought her from Saks Fifth Avenue. To match her fly, I wore a gold and black Versace shirt with the matching loafers and dress pants. We looked like royalty together. All heads turned when we stepped foot on the yacht. A few chicks were smiling and winking, but I had my woman. There was no need for another one.

I pulled out her chair and helped her get comfortable. "What you want to drink?"

"Champagne."

"I'll be right back." As I headed in the direction of the bar, I was sidestepped by one of the females that was checking me out.

"Oh, sorry. I didn't see you."

"It's all good." I proceeded to the counter. "Hey, my man, let me get a bottle of Moet."

"That'll be one hundred and sixty two dollars." He turned away to grab what I ordered then placed it on the counter.

I handed him the total amount plus a tip. "Keep the change."

Just as I turned around, the same woman was standing all in my personal space. "Lucky lady."

"Nah, I'm a lucky man. Have a good evening."

Throughout dinner, every time I looked up, that bitch was steady watching me. I had mad respect for women, but not hoes. And she was one of them hoes that wanted what they couldn't have.

"Don't look, but we have ourselves an admirer," I whispered in her ear.

"Is that right?"

"Yup! Give me a kiss since she wanna see something." Skai gave me some tongue action while everyone was sitting at the table eating.

The expression on her face was priceless. She looked away quickly and put her attention to the folks she was seated with.

After dinner was over, we spent a little time in their club area, enjoying the music and drinking. "Can we go out and get some fresh air? I have a headache."

"I think I got something for that."

"Oh yeah?"

"Indeed. I'll show you."

Skai and I walked to the outside and around the back. It was dark outside, but the moon and stars lit up the entire universe. Holding hands, we admired the view.

"Just a few months ago, the only thing I could stare at was the bottom of a rusty-ass bunk and barbed wires. Now look at me, standing on a muthafuckin' yacht, sippin' champagne with my beautiful queen. This shit feels so good. I never thought I would be doing any of this."

"I'm happy you're free and doing well. You deserve everything you have. I know you had it hard in there."

"Do I deserve you?"

"I'm standing here, aren't I?"

Skai hugged me and buried my head in her chest. "I love you, and I appreciate everything you did for me."

Lifting her up, I sat her on the bench and stood between her legs. Tears were streaming down her face. I wiped them away. "Don't cry. I love you too."

Kissing her, I pushed her dress to the side and sucked on her pearl tongue. My dick was so hard it was about to burst through my pants. Freeing him, I put him inside his nesting area. Holding her plump ass so she didn't slide, I pumped in and out of her slowly. I could hear light footsteps coming towards us, but I couldn't stop if I wanted to. The noise stopped and when I looked up, it was my stalker. She was watching me in awe, so I kept going so she'd have something to look at.

Skai's legs were wrapped around waist. She was panting softly, since I wasn't trying to rough house the pussy. Glancing towards our silent visitor, we locked eyes. "You like this, don't you?"

"I love this shit," Skai replied, although I was asking her. The woman finally walked away and that was the last I saw of her until we were getting off the boat.

Skai was aware of the stunt she pulled. As we walked past her and the dude she was with, Skai stopped and looked her up and down. The she looked at the dude.

"Excuse me. Is this your girlfriend?"

"Yeah."

"Well, just so you know she has been trying to get at my dude since we boarded. You should find you a woman. Not a hoe."

Her attention immediately went back to the female. "You see, this man right here belongs to me. He ain't doing no cheating, so I hope you enjoyed watching him fuck me. And when we get home, I am going to lick and suck that dick until he cums down my throat. Think about that while you home with your dude. Have a good night."

We both walked off laughing. Her craziness is what I loved the most about her. She was adamant about the one she loved. "Bae, you wild, man."

"I had to let that hoe know. Don't play with me. You off the market now, so it's too late for these hoes."

"Bae."

"Yes, my love?"

"You meant what you said about licking and sucking the dick until I cum down your throat?"

"Hell yeah! Just wait until we get home."

"Can we start in the car?"

"No sir. You have to wait on this fire head."

I tore up the highway trying to get back to the crib. My lady was the shit.

The End

SUPAFREAK

ASIA

It was the middle of the summer and the heat was kicking my ass. It had to be the hottest day of the decade. Here I laid half naked in my bed with only my bra and panties on, trying to keep cool. My box fan was circulating air, but that shit wasn't cold enough for me. The A/C unit in my building was fucked up and my sorry-ass landlord hadn't sent the maintenance man yet. He had another thing coming when the first of the month rolled around. If my shit wasn't blowing cold like ice, he wasn't getting shit.

Sleep was the best thing going right now, but I was too horny to do that. Scrolling through my call log, I hit up my cut buddy Torey.

"What's good?"

"Thinking about you. What you doing?" I rocked my legs, trying to cool down the fire between my legs.

"Chillin'."

"Come over here."

"I can't right now."

"Why not?"

"My baby mama in my ass today. She been like that since she saw the pussy pics you sent me."

"Boy, bye. She can't stop you from cheating."

"I know, but I don't feel like going through all that with her."

"Call me when she give you back your balls." Torey started laughing, but I didn't find shit funny, so I hung up on his lame ass.

"Well, Pinky, I guess it's me and you today." Pinky was my bullet and she never let a bitch down. Nor did she cheat.

Grabbing my toy from underneath the bed, I powered her on and pushed my panties to the side. Sliding it across my clit, my legs opened wider. "You a powerful little bitch too."

The strong vibrations sent shock waves up my vagina. I had it on the maximum level too. Seconds later, I was creaming all over the plastic. That only gave me temporary pleasure, but for now, that would do. On my way to the bathroom, I stopped and grabbed a new rag from the hall closet. After I washed my twat and vibrator, I went back into the room to put it away.

My mouth was dry as hell, so I went into the kitchen to fix something to drink. Snatching the box open, I huffed. "It ain't shit in this muthafucka!"

Slamming the door, I waltzed my ass back into the room and threw on a pair of small shorts, tank top, and some slides. When I stepped outside, the heat slapped me in the face like *Hey, bitch, where you going?* The store was across the street, so I didn't have to drive.

A voice from behind startled me. "Hey sexy."

When I turned around, I was standing up close and personal with my ex-boyfriend, Steve. He was still fine as hell too with that brown skin and wavy hair. His teeth were pearly white at the top and gold at the bottom. "Where the hell you come from?"

"I just moved back into town. How have you been?"

"I'm good."

"Still looking good, I see."

"You already know." I was blushing hard as hell.

"Where you headed?"

"To the store."

"Let me give you a ride. It's hot as hell out here."

The sun was shining directly in my face and I was sweating like a pig on a roaster. We walked to a Chevrolet Impala and got in. "You know I been looking for you?"

"Is that right?"

"Yeah."

"You know I don't believe that."

"Why not? You were my first love."

Sucking my teeth, I laughed it off. "Boy, please. You know I don't believe that."

"That's cool." Steve pulled up at the corner store and passed me a fifty dollar bill. "Get what you want. Just bring me a Gatorade back."

"Okay." I got out of the car and went inside.

Upon my return, I saw that Steve was on the phone, but he was talking on speaker. "How much you need?"

"One fifty."

"Give me ten minutes and I'll be there."

"Don't be lying, nigga, I know you. Ten minutes means forty."

"Nah, I'm coming to you right now. I'm at the store on Nineteenth Street."

"I'm waiting."

"Bet." He hung up the phone and set it in his lap. "You wanna ride with me somewhere?"

"I'm already in the car. Go ahead."

Steve drove us to the Washington Park neighborhood and got out of the car. To keep me entertained, I went on Facebook to see what bitches was on there lying about and sipped on my tea. Ten minutes passed and he was getting back in the car.

"Here's your change."

"Keep it, and if you stick around. It'll be more where that came from."

Sticking the money back in my pocket, I nodded my head. "We'll see about that. You do a lot of talking and no action."

"That's the past. Let that go."

"It's only been what, two years?"

"Yeah, but I changed."

"Like I said, we'll see. For the record, I'm not holding my breath on that one."

"Damn! You ain't got no faith in a nigga."

"The last time I had faith in you, what happened?"

"I was younger then. Still immature. I'm a grown-ass man now."

"Well, that should be a walk in the park for the grown man."

Steve turned the music up high and headed back to my place. When we got back there, he parked facing the fence and turned the music down. Then he looked at me. "What's on your mind?"

"Nothing. Why, what's on your mind?"

Steve licked his lips. "Honestly." He paused. "I wanna eat that pussy."

Shiidd, he ain't have to tell me twice. "It's hot in there. My landlord didn't fix my air conditioner."

"I'll eat that muthafucka right here." He grabbed my shorts and tried to loosen them, so I did it for him. "Climb in the back." Steve got in the back seat and locked the doors.

Leaning against the passenger door, I propped one leg on the arm rest. Steve went in head first. His licks and slurps were loud and hella sloppy. It felt good though. Holding his head in place, I threw my pussy in his face, smearing my juices everywhere.

Steve stopped eating me out and pulled me towards him by my legs. Pulling his pants down to his knees, he whipped his dick out and put it in my pussy. "Put your other leg on the seat so I can dig all up in this."

Car sex was raunchy as hell, but I loved that shit. There was nowhere to run and I could feel it all. Moving my leg, I planted it firmly against the window. Steve was humping on me hard and dripping sweat onto my face. "Grip my dick."

Clenching my muscles, I squeezed down on his dick. I did it a few times, then stopped. "Keep doing it."

Steve kept pumping and the car kept rocking. If anyone walked past it, they would know what was going down, but I didn't give a fuck. I was trying to get my rocks off. Pinching my clit, I twirled it between my fingers.

"Make me nut," I whispered. "Fuck this pussy harder."

Steve banged me up in that back seat like he ain't had sex in a while. "Raise your shirt. I'm finna nut."

I moved my shit in the nick of time because, he pulled out right after that and jacked his dick. Thick white snot was all over my stomach.

"Really, bruh?"

"Shit!" He took a deep breath. "I told you I was nutting."

"Help me up. I'm stuck."

Steve pulled me up and sat back. "My damn back hurt."

"You chose to do it in here."

"That's 'cause you ain't want me to come in. You thought I was gon' try and spend the night."

"No, you could've." That meant all night dick for me. I was still backed up.

"Word?"

"Yeah."

"When they fixing your air?"

"I don't know, but it better be fast. I'm tired of being hot."

"I'll get you a room until they fix it."

That sounded good to me. "You will?"

"Yeah. Go pack some clothes and come on."

"Okay." Once I put my shorts back on, I got out and packed a few outfits and my personal items.

***

Steve

We checked in at the Extended Stay in Tamarac and went upstairs. I chose a smoking room so I could smoke in peace. Asia went in the bathroom to take a shower while I rolled up a few blunts. I knew she liked to smoke, so I made sure I had enough for the both of us. My cell phone buzzed on the dresser, so I answered it.

"Hello."

"Where you at, bruh?"

"I'm off in the cut chillin'. What's up?"

"I needed some trees."

"Shit, I'm out the area right now. If I come back on that side, I'll slide up on you."

"A'ight."

"Yeah."

While I smoked a blunt, I played some music on my phone. A nigga was trying to vibe. Whoever didn't grab trees and coke before I disappeared was shit out of luck until I got back on that side of town. The purpose in me going far was so that I could chill in peace with Asia. If she decided to take me back, I was gon' move out my baby mama's shit ASAP. We weren't together or nothing like that. She just let a nigga crash on the sofa when I got back. I hit her a few times, but

I didn't want her. My phone vibrated again and it was her. Speak or think of the devil and they would always appear.

"Yeah."

"Bring me some food when you come home."

"I'm out the area right now."

"Well, when you coming home?"

"I'm not."

Asia walked out wearing a towel. "You gon' take a shower?"

"Who the fuck you with?" My baby mama was screaming loud through the receiver, so I played it off and hung up the phone. Hopefully Asia didn't hear that. I'd just tell her my phone died.

"Yeah, in a minute." Hitting the blunt, I passed it to her.

"You want this?"

"Yeah." Asia grabbed it and took a few pulls.

"I'm going to hop in the shower."

Standing underneath the shower head, I let the water splash all over my face and body. After soaping up the washcloth, I scrubbed my body clean and rinsed off. Stepping onto the towel that was on the floor, I wrapped my bottom half with a towel and walked out. Asia was higher than a muthafucka. She was on her back, sprawled across the bed. Her head hung slightly off the bed.

Dropping my towel to the floor, I stood over her and rubbed my thick member across her slightly open mouth. She smacked her lips and opened her eyes.

"Why you standing over me?"

"Open your mouth."

Asia complied with my freaky request. That was an invitation to have my way with her. Squatting down, I shoved my dick into her mouth. Dipping low, I moved up and down. Then I planted one foot on the bed. Asia's mouth glistened as the pre-cum oozed from my tip. The corners of her mouth accumulated more spit with each stroke.

"Spit on it. Make that shit nasty and wet."

Asia palmed my scrotum, making my knees grow weak and worked her throat muscles. The suction on her mouth was tight like a vacuum. It didn't take long for my blood-filled shaft to prepare for a shoot off. Pulling it out of her mouth, she popped her lips.

"Suck my balls," I demanded.

Tea bagging was my style. Some stripper chick turned me on to that and I fell in love with that shit. Asia took my balls into her mouth and did that hiccup motion. She had to know it felt good because she didn't stop. As she stroked my dick fast, that nut resurfaced and erupted like a volcano. My babies covered her face and mouth, but she licked it clean.

I was done for the night, but she wasn't. Mounting up, she got on top and rode me in reverse.

My phone was vibrating, so I reached over and grabbed it. There were multiple text messages from my baby mama cursing me out. I wasn't trying to hear that shit, so I cleared them out and opened up my camera. The sight of my dick gliding in and out of some wet pussy was all I wanted to see.

The End

Destiny Skai

EVEN SWAP AIN'T NO SWINDLE

FOREIGN

As I stood looking in the mirror, I wiped my tears away. My heart was completely torn into two pieces. Mentally, I wasn't okay and I could feel myself diving completely off the edge. My husband of three years was having an affair, and he had no couth about himself whatsoever. The hoodrats he chose to sleep with were social media attention seekers and would do anything for a buck and a fuck. Over and over, he showed me that he had no regards for our marriage.

Aaron Young was the love of my life and I knew that the moment my best friend and his twin sister, Alexis Young, introduced us in high school. We all attended Bethune Cookman College so we could stay together. Everything was good with us until he was drafted to the NFL. That's when the groupies showed up and sent my world tumbling in a downward spiral.

Although he was the ultimate cheater, I stayed because I loved him and thought he would change. You'd think after two miscarriages he would get his shit together, but unfortunately, he was too selfish to consider my feelings. I was used to the cheating, but what I didn't expect was for one of those thirsty thots to send me a video of my husband feasting between her legs. It pained me to see him giving her oral pleasure when he had a problem with oral sex in the first place.

The door slammed, signaling his return. Opening up my phone, I set it to play. Aaron walked through our master bedroom with a smile on his face, without a care in the world. He dropped his duffle bag and stepped to me.

"How is my beautiful wife?" He attempted to kiss me, but I curved him like a fast ball.

"Keep those unfaithful, dirty-ass lips away from me." I mugged him hard.

"What are you talking about? I haven't done anything."

"Oh, I beg to differ." I shoved the phone in his face. He grabbed it and backed up.

"What's this?"

"Hit play and you'll see."

Aaron touched the screen with his finger. After a few seconds, he threw the phone onto the bed and grabbed me. "I'm sorry. That's not what it looks like."

"Oh, really?" I reached back and slapped his face with all of the strength I had left in me. "It looks like my husband was eating pussy that doesn't belong to him."

"Let me explain," he pleaded.

"There's nothing to explain, Aaron. These are receipts. This is you on this video. I'm tired of this, I really am. You have me so tempted to walk away while I still have my sanity."

Aaron sat on the bed with his head hung low, rubbing his head like he was about to rub the hair off. "I don't know what's wrong with me. It's like I'm addicted to sex and I can't stop, no matter how much I try."

"That's no excuse. You let the money, fame, and these groupie hoes get in the way of everything we built. I'm non-existent in your world. You only need me around to cook your food, clean your house, and wash your clothes."

"That's not true, Foreign. I love you. That's why I married you." He attempted to be emotional, but his eyes were dryer than the Sahara Desert.

"You married me because you know that I'll never fuck you over. I take care of home and I don't party at all. You wanted a home body to raise your fuckin' kids and be a maid while you sling community dick all over the place. And why don't we have kids?" If he said anything slick, I was going upside his head.

Aaron looked in my eyes without an ounce of compassion. "I should be asking you that. I'm not the one whose body keeps rejecting them."

I grabbed the closest thing in my reach. That just so happened to be a perfume bottle. I threw it at him and clunked him upside the head. "It's your fault we don't have kids. Did you forget about the two miscarriages I had stressing and fighting these bitches because of your lying, deceitful ass?"

Aaron sat there looking like a deer in the headlights. "I didn't mean that."

"Don't apologize, because you meant every single word." There was so much rage and anger in my system. I wanted his ass to hurt the same way I was hurting. Give him a taste of his own medicine. Grabbing my keys and purse, I headed towards the door, then stopped.

"Just so you know, I'm done with this. I'm done crying and being sad. It's time that I start living my life as a single woman. I'm not enough for you and apparently, I'll never be."

"Where are you going?"

"That's none of your concern, dear. Why don't you question the bitch in the video? Don't wait up."

My outburst had me feeling like a new woman. It was about time I gave him a piece of my mind. It wasn't like I wasn't an attractive woman. If I must toot my own horn, I had to admit that I was fine. I was twenty-five years old, my complexion was pecan tan, my ass was nice, and my stomach was flat as a board. My body didn't have an ounce of fat on it. And yet that still meant nothing in my husband's eyes.

Today I was flaunting my shape in a casual jean dress that hung off the shoulders and nude strappy heels. Fashion Nova was my favorite place to shop. I wasn't big on designer. Materialistic things didn't mean shit to me. I was a simple girl. Aaron was the only one big on splurging. When he bought me the Bentley coupe for my birthday I was grateful, but he could've spent that money on a Toyota and I would've been satisfied.

Anyway, I unlocked the doors on my fancy whip, put on my shades, and took off out of the driveway. Tonight was about me, and I was looking to have some fun, even if I had to party alone. Ironically, that's what happened and I ended up at a karaoke spot.

Sitting at the bar, I made myself comfortable and ordered a Rum Runner. From my seat, I danced to the music and did my best to have a good time. Aaron called me twice, but I ignored both calls. And I did not send him a text. That bastard needed to wonder about my location for a change.

The DJ played "Twerk" by the City Girls, and that pulled me right off that stool. While I was dancing, some guy came behind me and grinded against my ass. Normally, I would've objected to it, but not that time. That night was all about me, and it felt good to receive attention from a man. When the song came to an end, I was sweaty as hell, so I went back to the bar. Dude was on my heels.

"You got moves out there on that dance floor."

He was handsome, to say the least. With that chocolate skin and white teeth, he resembled Morris Chestnut. "You not too bad yourself. Let me buy you a drink."

"Okay. Let me go to the ladies room and freshen up."

"I'll be waiting." He grinned, showing all thirty-two.

The restroom was empty when I stepped inside and as usual, someone was in there with a basket full of hygiene items you could use for a small fee. Passing on all her offers, I cleaned my face and went back to the door. Hershey Chocolate was sitting there waiting, as promised.

Damn, he could cover me in his chocolate any day.

That was the liquor talking, of course. Being the gentleman that he was, he helped me into my seat and ordered me a second drink.

"So what's a beautiful woman like you doing in here alone? Trouble in paradise?" He nodded his head towards my huge wedding ring.

"You can say that."

"I guess he doesn't realize how lucky he is." He sipped his Courvoisier on the rocks.

"You'll be guessing right."

"That's unfortunate. You're truly a prize."

"You don't even know me," I replied sassily, sipping from my straw.

"I'm naturally drawn to good people. Besides, for you to be off the market means he saw something special in you."

"That's what I thought in the beginning."

We continued to have small talk and order more drinks. By my third cup, Maurice had the waitress bring us two shots a piece. The both of us were tore the hell up. Maurice stood up and gave me a lap dance. It was so funny. I loved his energy. The room started to spin a little, so I had to sit down for a few.

"You okay?"

"Yeah. I just felt dizzy all of a sudden."

Maurice ordered me a bottled water. I downed that quickly. "I need another one." After I drank some of the second one, I sat for a bit and the room was now at a standstill. On my feet, I grabbed my purse.

"Going to freshen up?" he asked.

"I'm going home now. I need my bed."

"Let me walk you out."

"It's okay. I can manage."

"I want to make sure you make it to your car safely."

"Okay."

My car was parked in the front, so I didn't have far to walk. Stopping beside the door, I placed my hand on his firm chest. "This is me right here. Thank you."

Maurice opened my door. "So can I have your number?"

"Is this you shooting your shot?" I giggled.

"Not really. I just - " Then he shook his head. "Guilty."

"I don't think that's a good idea. I did have a good time. Thank you."

"Well, take my number just in case you need someone to talk to."

"Okay." Maurice locked his number in my phone and I pulled off.

Halfway down the street, I became nauseous. I attempted to hold it so I could pull over. But it was too late because I hurled over in the passenger seat, regurgitating on the floor. "Shit!"

Now I had this big-ass mess to clean. My car was going to be funky as hell once the sun came up. Halfway home I remembered there was a late night car wash, so that's where I went. Surprisingly, they were still there. There were two vehicles being cleaned, so I parked in the guest spot.

As I walked up, I was greeted by one of the attendants. "We're closing in thirty minutes."

"Sorry, but I have an emergency. My friend threw up in my car and I need to have it cleaned before it settles in my carpet.

"That's a lot of work and we won't make it."

Just as I was about to walk away, I was stopped by something tall, brown, and handsome. The broadness in his shoulders stood out, just like the bulging print in his joggers. *Damn!*

"Excuse me, Miss. What do you need?" His baritone voice made my kitty squirm.

"Um. I. Um. I need a car wash. My girlfriend had one too many drinks and threw up in my front seat."

"We can take care of that for you. Give me your keys."

He then tossed them to his worker. "Wash the lady's car. Be a gentleman, fool." Then he looked back at me. "Follow me."

Yassss! Lead me into the land of the living. I'd follow his sexy ass to the moon if that's where he was going. We walked inside the building.

"You can wait in my office. I know you don't want to sit out in that humid air."

"Thank you."

"I'm Demerius, but my friends call me Domestic."

We shook hands. "Nice to meet you. I'm Foreign."

"That's an interesting name."

"So is yours, and blame my mama for that one."

"It suits you." He pulled my seat out for me. "I'll be back."

"Okay."

The liquor had me a little spaced out and I couldn't wait to get home and dive head first into my bed. His office air was blowing hard and I needed all the air I could get.

Domestic came back fifteen minutes later and sat down behind his desk. My guess was that he was doing some work by the way he was studying his computer.

The silence was killing me, but I didn't want to interrupt, so I kept myself busy by reading a book on Kindle. After a while he looked up.

"I apologize. I'm trying to log my receipts for the day. I swear I need an assistant."

My eyes met his. "No apology necessary. Business is important. I'm okay."

"Many women don't understand that."

"I'm not like other women."

Leaning back in his seat, he folded his hands. "Why you outside this time of night?"

"Well, if you must know, I was out having drinks with my girlfriend."

"Right." He smiled, shaking his finger. "You did say that, but if you were my woman, you'd be locked down in the house."

"Well, thank God I'm not."

"I'd do something about that slick tongue too."

"And what exactly would you do with my slick tongue, Mr. Demerius?" That liquor had me bold.

"I'll bite on it and suck it. You'll be at my mercy." He licked his lips and I almost creamed in my panties. I was too excited.

"Hmm. I guess."

His worker walked in. "Aye, boss. We all done out here. I'm leaving. Tony gon' finish up her car. It should be done in thirty minutes or so."

"I'm coming out. I'll be right back." He excused himself.

"Um. Where is your bathroom?"

"Down the hall. I'll point you in the right direction."

My bladder felt like it was about to explode at any minute. Quickly, I hiked up my dress and squatted over the toilet. The release of that hot piss brought on so much relief. Afterwards, I cleaned up with my Summers Eve wipes and washed my hands. As I strolled down the hall, Demerius was returning to his office. And Lord have mercy, this man was not wearing a shirt, exposing those beefed up muscles. It was definitely time to leave the premises.

"Everything good?" He smiled. That was when I realized he had a dimple in his left cheek.

"Of course."

"Good."

My eyes were zoomed in on his beautiful tattoos and smooth caramel skin. The man was a fine piece of male specimen. Saliva stirred around my mouth. Swallowing hard, I cleared my throat. He caught me staring.

"You like what you see?" His ole cocky ass.

"Maybe," I stated boldly.

Demerius walked over and stood in front of me. Grabbing my hand, he placed it on his chest and made it jump. The slightest touch of him made my kitty jump around in my panties. I wanted to move my hand so bad, but it was stuck in place. Thoughts of Aaron flashed through my mind. I didn't want to be like him and break my wedding vows. Picking up my purse, I stood up.

"I have to go. Is my car ready?"

"Not yet. Why you in a rush?" Demerius placed his hand underneath my dress and traced my panty line with his finger. Firmly, he gripped my ass and gave it hard squeeze. "I like you."

His hands were quite frisky as he made his way to the front. The tips of his fingers grazed my lips and I melted fast like butter.

"You don't know me."

"We can change that." Demerius rolled his tongue across the side of my neck. On contact, my eyes closed and I placed my hands on his waist. *Fuck it!* Aaron wasn't being faithful to me, so fuck him.

To soothe my curious mind, I placed my hand on his crotch and squeezed it. He has semi-hard. I had to make sure he was working with something worth cheating with. The harder he sucked on me, the wetter the seat of my panties got.

"Fuck me!" I whispered.

Placing his strong hands on my ass, he scooped me up and sat me on his desk. He removed my panties and threw them. "Spread them legs for me."

"Close the door first." I didn't want anyone to walk in and witness what was about to go down.

"Don't worry, everybody gone."

"What about my car?"

"It been ready. I wanted to spend more time with you." Pushing my legs further apart, he stroked my whole cat with his hand. "Oh yeah, she shaved too."

Demerius arched his back and became face to face with my plump peach. His nose was all up in it, doing what I assumed to be the smell test. Using his fingers, he separated my lips and sucked on my pulsating bud. It hardened when it came in contact with his thick lips. The flick of his tongue made my body shutter. He confirmed he was a stone cold freak when he put my legs on his shoulder, lifted my ass up, and licked me from the back to the front and stopping at my Hershey Highway.

"Ssss. Mmm. Yessss!"

Demerius sucked on my lips individually and kissed them gently. Removing his joggers, I watched closely as they dropped. That nigga was hung like a horse. Looking me in my eyes, he stroked it. My eyes widened just a bit. He was packing more than Aaron, without a doubt.

"You can handle all this beef?"

"I guess we're about to find out."

Snatching me to the edge and teasing my entrance, he soaked his head with my juices. Forcing his length inside, he gripped my hips and pushed hard until he sunk deep into my ocean.

"Ahhhh shit!" I yelped while wrapping my legs around his waist.

"You feel this fat-ass dick in that sweet pussy?"

"Yes. Yes."

My pipes definitely needed cleaning out because I wasn't sleeping with my husband every night. I put his ass on restriction two weeks ago. Every time he rammed his Mandingo-sized meat up in me, I could feel pressure in my ass, like he was fucking me from the front and the back at the same time. My first thought was, *This man is about to kill me in here*. Wrapping my arms around his neck, I clamped him tight.

"Lay back and spread them legs. I'on wanna see nothing but pussy."

With my back resting on his desk and my legs stretched north and south, Demerius propped one leg on the desk and drove is big ass long rod deep inside my snatch box. "Fuccckkk!"

He went crazy, bouncing up and down in my shit. Demerius drilled me hard. His heavy balls slapped me against my ass with every stroke.

"Ooooh! You killing me!" I cried.

"Take this fat dick." He put his hand on my stomach and pushed down on it. My moaning got louder. "Say my name while I beat this pussy up."

"Demerius!" I shouted.

"No! Call me Domestic."

"Domestic!" I screamed.

"Uh huh. Just like that."

Demerius was grunting and fucking me like a madman. "I don't give a fuck who you married to. This my pussy now."

What! I thought.

Domestic played with my clit, rubbing her fast. A pleasurable amount of pressure built up inside of me. Yep, my orgasm had surfaced and I was ready to erupt. "Oooh shit, I'm cumming. Ssss. It's cumming. Shit. Keep going. Beat this pussy."

"Whose shit this is?"

"Yours," I complied.

"Damn right. Say that shit."

"Domestic. Domestic. I'm cumming."

"Bust then."

The both of us came at the same time and just like that, my little sexcapade was over. However, I didn't want it to end. There would be more where that came from.

"Your husband fucked up now. You ain't going nowhere."

Playing hard, I smirked. "Oh really?"

"You goddamn right." Demerius got dressed and helped me off his desk. "Lock my number in your phone. You'll be hearing from me tomorrow morning."

I did like I was told. Demerius kissed me on my cheek and escorted me to my vehicle. "Get home safe, baby. Shoot me a text so I can sleep comfortably knowing you made it in one piece."

"I will."

When I got home, I was cheesing my ass off. All I wanted to do was shower and go to sleep. My body was tired and needed some rest.

Aaron was sitting up in bed watching television. Deep down I wanted to laugh so bad because he looked just like me when I waited on him to come home at night. Pitiful.

"Where you been?"

"Out."

"With who?"

"Why? You don't get to question me."

"I'm the man of this house and you will tell me where you been," he barked angrily.

"I'm not telling you shit. How about that?" I walked off and went in the bathroom and sent Domestic a text message as requested.

One month later

Domestic and I had been kicking it heavy, and I do mean every aspect of the word. Many of my days were spent at his carwash. Instead of hiring a personal assistant, he had me working there instead, and with pay. I didn't need it, but I sure as hell wasn't turning it down. Whenever it slowed down and he could squeeze in a break, he would come into the office and give me the business. On the desk, the chair, and on the floor. We didn't discriminate when it came time to get down and dirty. He even took me to his house a few times, and it was gorgeous.

The carwash he had was only one of three. I found that out when he allowed me to accompany him during the pick-ups. Come to find out he was thirty-eight, which made him thirteen years older than me, with a fourteen-year-old son that lived with him. I was cool with that though. Then he mentioned that he wanted to have another child.

Things at home started to change when I became absent. Aaron was no longer staying out late or attending those wild parties. I knew the sudden shift was an attempt to suck me back in so that he could resort back to his old ways. This time it wasn't happening because I was happy with Domestic and what we had going on. I was completely stress free and I loved it.

After a long hot shower, I hopped in bed. Aaron wasn't home yet, which was fine with me. That was my chance to go to sleep before he arrived. What a fool I was, because no sooner did I have that thought than he was coming into the bedroom.

"Foreign," he called out, but I didn't respond. "I know you're not asleep."

Aaron sat on my side of the bed. As bad as I wanted to pretend to be asleep, I knew he wasn't going to move until I said something.

"What?"

"We need to talk."

"I'm sleepy. We can talk tomorrow."

"No. We need to talk now."

Opening my eyes, I pouted. Just so he would know how irritated I was with his presence. "What?"

"You're changing."

"You don't say," I replied sarcastically.

"I'm losing you and I don't want to. We need to fix this before it gets too deep."

That was just like a typical cheating, no good-ass man. They loved to dish shit out, but could never take it. "It's been deep, Aaron. Where the hell have you been for the past three years? Oh, I forgot. You were too busy fucking every Tasha, Kim, and Stacy. I'm tired and I don't want to hear this shit. Now if you don't mind, I would like to go to bed."

"I'm not giving up on us."

Aaron left the room and went into the bathroom. Time passed and I must've dozed off. When I opened my eyes, Aaron was between my legs trying to give me head. Closing my legs, I snapped. "What are you doing?"

"I want to make love to my wife."

"Well, I don't want it."

Aaron pushed my legs out the way. "Who the fuck is he?"

"Who is who?"

"The nigga you been fuckin', that's who. For the last month and a half, you've made zero attempts to have sex with me, and when I try, I get the same reaction."

"Let's see. Maybe I'm tired of getting sloppy seconds. You out fucking these random bitches and then you come home to me like I'm your side chick. I don't think so."

"Whatever you got going on, end it now, I'm not playing with you."

Aaron rolled over and went to sleep. If he thought I was ending shit with Domestic, he had another thing coming. That man wrote his name in cursive on this pussy, and that was who it belonged to. If he thought he was hurt now, his shit was gon' split in a million pieces when he found out I was pregnant with another man's baby.

The End

Destiny Skai

HIS BONNIE, HER CLYDE

BLAZE

My feet hit the pavement at one hundred miles per hour. I didn't have on a single pair of shoes, but my bag was secure across my back as I ran for my life. My attacker could be heard, but not close enough to catch me.

"Blaze, stop! 'Cause when I catch you, bitch, I'ma kill yo' ass."

I ignored the threats of my ex-boyfriend Terrell and kept on pushing. Because if he thought I was about to stop, he had life all fucked up. I escaped for a reason, and there was no looking back. My body was in pain from the ass whooping he put on me just minutes ago. He was my king in the beginning, but all he turned out to be in the end was a peasant, a fuck boy, in my eyes. Any man that beat on a woman got zero respect from me, so I had to escape from his brutal ways. No matter how many designer shades he put on my face to cover the black eyes, the pain wasn't worth it, so I bounced. The only time I liked my face beat was when I stepped out to grace the world with my presence.

Never in a million years did I think track would ever play a role in my life after graduation. Thank God for the little things in life, such as sports. My feet were burning on the concrete and I just knew I would tumble over face first at any moment. Dying wasn't an option, so I had to keep on pushing. I didn't know where I was running to because I wasn't from Tennessee, nor was my ex. He was a check boy, so we normally bounced from state to state, living the high life.

Just when I thought I was running on a path to nowhere, I saw a curb coming up and I bent it quickly, making a mad dash down the alley. I had to pick up the pace because I was finally out of his sight. I continued to run until I saw a dumpster I could hide behind. I squatted down and fumbled through my bag for my cell phone, but I couldn't find it. What I did find was a semi-automatic that belonged to Terrell. He must've forgotten to take it out of my bag and that was another blessing, because if he pursued me any further, I was gon' knock his lights out. I could hear him calling out to me once again.

"Blaze!" he shouted. "Come out, baby. I'm sorry I hit you. I promise I won't do it again."

That was a lie because I had heard it all before. I sat behind the dumpster for at least a good thirty minutes before I came out of hiding. I clutched the weapon in my hand and proceeded down the alley. I just knew at any moment he would grab me from behind. The alley was dark and scary that time of night and it reeked of hot piss, garbage, and sewer water. There were good times with Terrell, but the bad definitely outweighed that. Try sleeping with a broken heart every night and the man that was supposed to love you was kicking your ass on the regular and was the reason for your miscarriage. Hell could freeze over twice and I still wouldn't take his ass back.

As I continued on my journey I froze up at the sudden noise behind me. My heart was beating at an unusual rate. When I did an about face quickly with the gun drawn and ready to blast, to my surprise, it was only a fucking possum. That shit gave me the creeps, so I walked a little faster. My feet were soaked in contaminated shit water and Lord knows I couldn't wait to get a shower.

I had no idea how I was going to get back to Florida, but I needed to think fast. The little bit of money I had would only get me a room for one night and after that, I was fucked. "Where is my guardian angel when I need one?"

Suddenly I approached a window and I could hear some talking. I stood on my tippy toes to get a better look inside. There were a few guys sitting at a table playing cards for money. I walked around to the front and knocked on the door. Moments later, some fat dude opened the door and looked me up and down.

"How can I - " He paused when he got a good look at my battered face and black eye. "Are you okay?" he asked politely.

I forced a few tears from my eyes. "My boyfriend is trying to kill me. Can I use your phone?"

He reached in his pocket and pulled out his cell. "Here. go 'head."

"Can I come in please? I don't want him to see me."

"Sure."

I grabbed his phone and stepped inside, pretending to make a call. The inner child in me prayed for a peaceful ending, but the gangster in me went into survival mode. As soon as he turned his back, I pulled my strap from my pocket and pushed it in his back. "Keep your hands where I can see them. I don't want to shoot you." He raised his hands in the air. "Now take me to the card game."

The fellas in the back were laughing and smoking cigars until we entered the room. I pushed big boy towards the crowd and he stumbled. "I want everyone to take off all of your valuables and put them on the table."

One man sucked his teeth. "Damn, we getting robbed by a female?"

I tooted my nose at him and pointed the pistol. "You damn right. Now do what I say before I make an example out your ass."

"My cell phone too?"

"Duh."

Everyone amongst the crowd were older, but there was one that stuck out like a hang nail. He didn't look like he belonged with the crowd at all. Dude was definitely a beautiful sight for these sore eyes. He smiled at me and took off his watch, throwing it on the table. I waved the gun at him.

"Put all of this stuff in that plastic bag over there."

Sexy got up and did as he was told, and that smile never left his face. It made me wonder if he was turned on by being robbed or some shit. "Should I bring it to you?"

"Nah, slide it over here." Dude must have thought he was dealing with a fool or some shit. Sexy slid the bag and went back to his seat. "Alright, now put your heads down on the table and I'm going to leave."

As soon as their heads hit the table, I ran for the door. Once again I was back on the run, running for my life. After a good twenty miles, I ended up at the train station, but they were closed. I didn't know what I was gon' do now. There was no way to get out of Dodge and if I couldn't get away, I would be booked by morning, and that was a known fact.

My legs were tired of moving and I was out of breath, so I sat down on the bench to rest for a few minutes before going to look for the closest motel. During my break, I must've fallen asleep. When I opened my eyes, a man was tapping me on the shoulder. I jumped up with the gun in my hand, ready to squeeze every shell until there was none left.

"No, no, don't shoot," he pleaded.

To my surprise, it was Sexy from the gambling house. "Are you following me?" I asked.

"Yes and no."

"What the fuck does that mean?"

He held his hands up to show me he wasn't armed. "I'm not going to hurt you. 'Cause it looks like someone already did."

"I don't know that."

"Calm down and think for a minute." He pointed his finger at his temple. "You seem like a bright girl. If I wanted to hurt you, I could've done it while you were sleeping."

It made a little sense, but I wasn't buying it. "I guess so."

"Okay, listen. I'm going to reach into my back pocket to show you something."

"Don't try me, 'cause I will shoot you, and that's a promise."

He reached into his pocket and revealed a small black wallet. When he flipped it open, I almost died. Bright as the moon that shone over us was this bitch's police badge. My hands went to shaking and I dropped the gun, causing it to fire. We both dropped to the ground as it ricocheted off the concrete then into the wall. Seconds later we both got up and I turned my back towards him, interlocking my fingers behind my lower back.

"I know what time it is, so arrest me already. At least I know he can't kill me now."

The officer walked up behind me and I could feel his body heat. He was standing so close I could feel the bulging large print in his pants. His lips were on my ear. "Who did this to you?"

"My boyfriend." I sniffled. "Well, my ex-boyfriend now." I had to clear that up real quick.

Sexy grabbed my arm and turned me around so I could face him. "And that's why you just robbed us?"

"I'm not from here and I was scared. I didn't know what else to do to get money so I can go back home."

"What's your name?" he asked.

"Blaze."

"Is that your real name?"

"That's the name my mother gave me, and my birth certificate proves that fact."

"That's an interesting name, considering the fact that a woman pretty as you are is out wielding a gun and robbing folks." He laughed.

I didn't find the shit funny at all. "I'm glad you see the humor in this."

He nodded his head, but I didn't think he was buying that story. The cop pulled a knife from his pocket and I jumped back at least ten feet.

"Easy, cutie. I'm not gone hurt you." He walked away and used the knife to pluck the bullet from the wall. Looking over his shoulder, he smiled. "Come on, let's go, and don't forget to pick up your piece."

I picked up the gun and put it in my bag.

The drive was quiet, for the most part. He made small talk here and there. This man had me confused on more levels than one. For one, we were riding in an E-Class Benz, not a patrol car, and not once did he mention taking me to jail.

"Where are we going?"

"I have a hotel that I'm staying in, so we'll go there and figure out how I'm going to help you get away."

My eyes stretched far apart. "Help me? Why would you do that after what I did to you?"

"Well, technically you didn't do anything to me because you are going to give me back my watch and wallet. You can keep the money."

"Why would you do that?"

"A thank you would suffice."

He shut me up real quick. I looked down at the floor. "Thank you."

A few minutes later, we were pulling up to the Madison Hotel. When I walked in, I was floored by the Presidential suite. It was everything to me. The hardwood floors were gorgeous, but I was checking out the fully-stocked wet bar. I needed a drink badly, but I needed a shower more than anything.

"I really need a shower."

"Come on; right this way." I was escorted to the shower in the specialty suite.

I couldn't get over how nice the suite was and the fact he was in this big-ass room alone. "You're here alone. Why so much space?"

"My job paid me to come out here, so hey, why not splurge a little bit on their dime?"

"I agree with you on that." I smiled.

"Go ahead and take your shower and I'll bring you over a bathrobe. Put your clothes in one of those bags and I'll get those washed for you."

"Thank you."

After my shower, I wrapped myself in the robe and went to the living room. From the sounds of it, he was in the bathroom, so I took a seat until he returned. Minutes later, he walked out with a robe that only covered him from the waist down. He was so fine I almost passed out. Calling him sexy was an understatement. This man was cut everywhere and he had that dip to drive any woman crazy. My mouth watered at the sight.

He smiled at me with that gorgeous smile. "You look prettier than before."

I blushed. "You don't look too bad yourself."

"Come on, I could use a drink. How about you?"

Several drinks later I was on cloud ninety nine and pouring my heart out to a complete stranger. My tears were flowing heavy like the Mississippi River. He used his hand to wipe away my tears and once they were gone, our lips connected and electro waves took over my body. I couldn't resist the temptation inside of me. Not that I was trying to fight it either.

The chemistry between us was insane. He removed my robe, and then his. My eyes fell on his package, and I know he saw the fear in my eyes.

"Don't worry, I'll be gentle." He smirked.

He crept in the middle of my legs and entered me gradually. His length extended me and I lost my breath for a quick moment. I thought I was gon' kick the bucket at any minute. He took his time with me and long stroked me to death. The pain I felt subsided. Finally, I was able to relax and enjoy every inch of his fondant masterpiece.

With my legs up on his broad shoulders, he inclined forward, applying his body weight to my frame. Stuck in place, I was forced to take all nine to the tummy. "Ouuu! My stomach. My stomach." I was all out of breath and gasping for air.

The more I wailed, the deeper he went. He pounded my box with a little aggression, knocking the juice out. Placing my hand on his firm stomach, I attempted to slow him down. His pace was fast, like a power drill on the maximum speed. My ill nana was crying a river for him. She came so hard and long, I didn't think she would stop. Backing out the twat, he went down and slurped my juices. The magic stick made me cum five times in one night, and I knew he wasn't going nowhere.

The next day, he took me shopping and had me feeling like a new woman. We strolled through the mall hand in hand like we were the happiest couple on the planet. Inside his car, I sat and watched him get into the driver seat, and something finally crossed my mind. I looked him in those big, beautiful hazel eyes and he stared back at me, knowing something was wrong.

"You okay?" he asked.

"Yes. Something just crossed my name though."

"What's that?"

"You never told me your name."

He licked those thick, delectable lips. That traced lines all over my vagina as he replied smoothly, "They call me Gunz."

UNTAMABLE OBSESSION

Months had passed and Sahara's life was finally on track. She had recently opened up her own beauty bar with the help of Jayceon. He definitely kept his word and helped her get on her feet. Sahara was grateful for his help, although things didn't go as planned. He continued to come by the house and check on her and Jordan, as promised. Sahara was still not over the fact that she and Jayceon were over, so seeing him only made things worse. There was still a sense of hope that he would come to his senses and have a change of heart. She desperately craved the family life and she knew that it needed to be with him, but why? After all he'd said and done to her, she still couldn't let him go.

Sahara tried to convince herself that things were better off with the two of them apart and she should leave well enough alone, but her conscience wouldn't allow it. Her better judgment told her to be quiet and keep it to herself, so she did. Now on the flipside, Sahara still had the open case against her, but her attorney, Janet Rivers, promised that she wouldn't do another day in jail. It sounded good, but Sahara was a little skeptical. She knew what she was facing, but she wasn't about to admit that she was responsible for his death.

Tamela told her that if she wanted to get off, she would have to plead self-defense. At least they would have proof that she was a victim to his abuse. Sahara was undecided at the moment, so Tamela allowed her some time to think about it. She thought about it long and hard, but the decision should've been relatively simple: you go to jail or you go home. The choice is yours.

Sahara also had a confession to make, and it was eating her up on the inside, but there was no one she could talk too. Mya was definitely out of the question, and that's because she wasn't about to sugarcoat shit just to make her feel good. Now she could talk to Kayla because she knew that she could talk to her without judgment or ridicule, but that was too easy. And besides, Kayla didn't put her in the predicament that she was in. So why not go straight to the person that was responsible? None other than Jayceon himself.

Sahara thought about it for a few minutes, but so many thoughts were running through her head. It was difficult to continuously repeat what she'd been saying for the longest. However, the truth needed to come out and it needed to happen now. The hidden lie was literally suffocating her. It was so deep and heavy and her body was tired of carrying that burden like a Birken bag. If Sahara didn't come clean, she'd be sure to explode. Quickly deciding that it was now or never, she sent him a text message asking him to stop by the shop. Sahara was scared to death. This confession could turn out for the best or it could turn out really bad for her, but this was a chance she was willing to take. She waited patiently for his arrival.

One hour later, Jayceon was standing in front of the glass door. She took a deep breath as she let him in. Sahara noticed the same white Jeep that was there earlier, but she didn't mention it. Jayceon walked in happily, as if he had just gotten a free shipment of that white girl.

"What's going on?" he asked cheerfully.

"Nothing. You're awfully happy today. I should be asking you why you so happy?"

"No reason," he lied.

"Jayceon, I've known you for too long and I know when you lying, but that's okay, you don't have to tell me." Sahara laughed it off, trying to keep the atmosphere cool, calm, and collected with very little emotion.

"That's okay. I'll keep it to myself. It's not like you would care anyway."

Jayceon had piqued her interest and she wasn't stopping until she got an answer. "What is it? You might as well tell me. If it makes you happy, then I'm happy," she lied.

He wasn't going to say anything, but he knew that she wouldn't give up until he told her. "I just found out that I'm having a little girl." He was overly excited.

Jayceon wanted a daughter that he could spoil. He already had two boys. Sahara could've kicked herself for what she just said about his happiness because clearly that wasn't the truth by far. It showed on her face. Sahara thought that she would pass out at any moment. The room started to spin and her heart felt like it stopped beating. She felt like she was about to go crazy, but she was trying to keep her composure.

"Con-grat-u-lations." Her response sounded forced, as if someone was standing behind her twisting her arm.

The pain that she felt at the moment had to be the worst of all. Sahara wanted to lay down and die right then and there. Jayceon noticed the expression on her face, so he changed the subject.

"So what did you need to talk to me about?"

She led him to her office in the back. "We need to sit and talk about this." He was willing to be patient, so he sat down.

"So what's up?" he asked, as calm as could be.

Sahara could feel herself become emotional, but it was now or never. "I've been doing a lot of thinking."

As soon as those words left her lips, he knew that he was in for some shit that he didn't bargain for. Whenever she wanted to *talk*, an argument occurred right after. Jayceon's whole demeanor changed. His shoulders tensed up. He was no longer relaxed, only stiff as a board.

"Jayceon, I'm going through hell without you and I'm tired of not being with you. This whole thing is driving me crazy." He was speechless once again. "I love you so much and I don't want to be with anyone else. I can't pull myself to move on. I've turned down every man that has approached me, and it's because of you. I thought that you would come back to me."

A tear rolled down her cheek and she didn't bother to wipe it away. Jayceon had a blank expression on his face. He held his head back and rubbed his hands over his face and exhaled deeply. Sahara detected that he was mad, but when he spoke, he was still calm.

"Come on, Sahara, please don't do this to me right now."

"Don't do this to you?" she yelled. "What the fuck is that supposed to mean? Do you have any idea what I'm going through?"

Jayceon remained calm because he was well aware of her pain. He was more sympathetic than angry with her. "You're wrong, I do know how you feel. You must have forgotten that I was in your shoes a year ago. You had me damn near to yourself, but you couldn't decide. Did you forget about that?"

"What am I supposed to do without you?" she cried hysterically.

"I can't tell you what to do, but I can tell you this. I have no ill feelings toward you. And I will continue to be there for you like I said I would."

"You won't even fuck me anymore," she complained.

"Sex is not going to make the situation any better. That will only complicate things, and you know that we can't be together like that."

"Why?" she screamed.

Sahara was troubled and passionate, incapable of dealing with his dismissal. The agony he exposed her to caused a shortcoming to appear. She wasn't holding any punches. "Answer me!" she continued to yell.

Jayceon couldn't handle her in such a delicate state. He hated to see a woman cry and her emotions were tugging at his heart. He wanted to grab her and console her and tell her that everything would be okay, but he didn't have a choice. Jayceon knew he had to let things stay the way they were and let time heal all wounds.

"Jayceon, please say something?" she asked with tears in her eyes

Jayceon stood up to leave because watching her breakdown was like throwing salt into an open flesh wound. Sahara stood up in front of him. "Why can't you be with me?"

Jayceon couldn't look her in her eyes because he didn't want to hurt her more than he had already. Telling her the truth was like shooting himself in the foot, and he wasn't about to do that. His secret would definitely make her flip the fuck out.

"I just can't. I'm sorry."

Sahara began to cry and scream about the sacrifices that she made to be with him, only to have him walk away from her. She would not take another heartbreak without a battle. She was resolved to battle for her family.

"Calm down," he pleaded.

Sahara started to throw punches and go crazy on him. He managed to block some of her punches, but she did catch him in his lip, drawing blood, while continuing to scream. "Why? Tell me why?"

Jayceon felt the blood trickle from his lip and he became enraged. He grabbed her arms and shook her. "Stop it!" he yelled. "I can't take this shit from you anymore."

"Tell me why?" Sahara was trying to break free from his tight grip.

Out of nowhere he shouted, "I'm getting married."

Before he could catch those words, it was too late and he couldn't take it back. Sahara's body went numb as she thought about what he said to her.

Hurt and confused, she whispered. "You're what?"

"Nothing."

"You're getting married?" She sat down and cried her eyes out as Jayceon watched her closely.

"I'm sorry," he said sincerely.

"I can't believe that I went through all of that shit for nothing." Sahara looked at him with pure hate in her heart and eyes. He could feel her shooting daggers straight through him. If looks could kill, he would've been stretched out on the floor.

"I should've let you die." Her words were like venom, and he was utterly shocked. Sahara had never spoken to him like that before. She knew that her words stung, but she didn't care. He had brought her down to her knees for the last time, and it was because she allowed it.

"That's how you feel about me?" he asked, just above a whisper.

"I do now." She was so furious. Her brain couldn't process what was unfolding in front of her eyes.

Jayceon knew that she didn't really mean those words, but it was painful to hear them. He got up and headed to the door. "Is that all you had to say to me?" he asked out of curiosity.

"No!" she snapped. There was no need to hesitate with her answer. She had lost him already, so why not blow up his world? Sahara knew what she was about to say would change everything. The only thing unknown was if it was for better or worse.

Sahara looked him in his wicked eyes.

"I hate to bust your bubble, but you can stop thinking that she's having your first girl 'cause Jordan is your daughter."

Jayceon stood silent so he could digest what he had just heard. Sahara figured that maybe he would come to his senses and they could be together again. His facial expression did not match the words that flew from his mouth. His face was soft, but his words were poisonous.

"You expect me to believe that bullshit? You are amazing to me. First I tell you all of this, and now you want to spread a nasty lie like that. What the fuck is wrong with you? We can't and won't be together. And if you can't keep your composure, then maybe I should fall all the way back. I hate to put an innocent child in the middle of this, but her mama is tripping. I'm not about to go through this bullshit. I'm out of here, and don't call me either."

Jayceon was pissed. He jumped into his car and skidded off.

Feeling broken, confused, and worthless Sahara returned to her office to sulk. She pulled out her prescription bottle and dumped them eagerly into her hand. In seconds, the entire bottle had been discarded and everything around her went black.

Word got back to Jayceon that Sahara had attempted to commit suicide. Without hesitation, he ran to be by her side. The fact still remained the same. They couldn't be a couple, but he knew that his actions were to blame.

Sahara saw Jayceon walk into her room, but she pretended to be asleep. Just like him, this scene was also familiar. The last time she was there, he promised her that nothing had changed and he wanted to be with her more than ever. That turned out to be a lie. She was trusting that he would simply leave. His face was not the one she needed to see. It was because of his flaw that she was lying in that bed in any case. He simply needed to reveal to her that he was getting hitched. He couldn't have picked a superior time to drop the bomb on her and obviously she didn't pick a good time to tell him about his daughter either.

Sahara had never considered the fact that he was Jordan's father until Jordan's features began to change as she got older. One day he came to visit Sahara had taken a picture of the two of them together and she noticed similarities. She brushed it off as if her mind was playing tricks on her. She figured it was because she wanted him back. Her conscience wouldn't let it rest, so she referred back to her calendar and she realized that the dates didn't add up to what the doctor stated. The doctor clearly said that she was six months pregnant and not five.

Sahara was going to keep it a secret, but she figured Jordan shouldn't have to suffer the loss of a father when the real one was alive and well. They had made that bed and now she was determined to make him lie in it - even if it was against his will. She didn't care who it would hurt, and that included his baby mama, Cherish. That bitch was the main target since Sahara hated her with a passion. There was no way she was going to allow him to move on and live a happy life with that bitch while she suffered. Sahara was about to fuck his world up with no remorse. Cherish thought she was having Jayceon's first girl, but all hell was about to break loose.

All Sahara's life she watched men come and go out of her mother's life, and she wasn't about to let that happen to her. She had one boyfriend, and that was Santana, but now that he was gone, she needed a replacement. Growing up, every other night it was a different man, and Sahara didn't want to walk in her mother's footsteps. At the age of thirteen, she was pregnant with twins.

Jayceon finally decided that it was time to wake her up. He rubbed her back gently. "Sahara, wake up," he whispered. She moved around a little bit to make it seem like she was in a deep sleep. "Come on, get up."

She opened her eyes slightly. "What are you doing here?"

"I came to check on you."

"Why? It's not like you give a fuck anyway." She exhaled hard and rolled her eyes to let him know that she wasn't happy with his presence. "Who told you that I was here anyway?"

He totally ignored her bad attitude. All he wanted was answers and nothing else, but if she wanted to play nasty, he was ready. His mood was foul anyway.

"First of all, kill that attitude like this is not what you wanted in the first place. I know what you trying to do, and it ain't gon' work." He sat back and relaxed in the chair.

"Don't get too comfortable. I didn't ask you to come here."

"So you had Kayla call me up here for no reason, huh?" Of course he knew her friend had no part in that, but reverse psychology would probably work better on her.

"I don't know what you're talking about. I didn't ask nobody to call your ass."

"I'm sure this was all a part of your little plan." He was trying to push her buttons, and it worked.

"What plan?" she shouted. "If you think that I'm trying to trick or trap you, you better think again, because it's not that serious."

"Who are you trying to convince? We both know that's a lie." He was cocky when he spoke. Jayceon knew at any given moment he could have her back. All he had to do was say it and she would come running. "So tell me this…" he paused. "Why are you here?"

"It doesn't matter."

"It doesn't matter if you live or die?"

"Nope."

"Did you forget about your daughter?"

"You don't care about her, and besides, she doesn't need me. I'm unstable."

"Are you even listening to yourself? What is wrong with you?"

"Just leave. Go check on your baby mama."

"Why are you giving me so much grief? I don't understand you."

Sahara sat up in the bed. "You got to be fucking kidding me! I know you didn't just say that." She couldn't believe the words that fell from his lying lips.

"What?"

"Don't play games with me, Jayceon. Are you listening to yourself?"

"Actually, I am."

"Clearly you're not, if you believe your own lies."

He sat up in the chair. Believe it or not, she was quite the character and he was enjoying the dumb role she was playing. She acted as if she had no part in the reason they weren't together.

"You need to calm down before they call security in here."

"Fuck you and security!"

"Is that how you feel?"

"Yes."

"No you don't."

"And what makes you think that?"

He held his arms out. "Well, this isn't exactly the Doubletree."

She was clearly disgusted with his sarcasm. "Go to hell."

"That's exactly where you're going if you kill yourself."

"Get the fuck out of my room. I hate you!" she yelled as she pointed to the door.

"I didn't mean that. I'm sorry." He walked up to her and held her tight in his arms. "I didn't mean any of that."

After all the hurtful shit he just said, there was no way in hell she was about to hug him back. It took all her strength to keep her from breaking down in that room. Sahara kept her head down as the tears fell from her eyes.

"Yes, you do."

"Come on, you know that I hate to see you cry."

"Yeah, right, because if that was true, you wouldn't make me cry."

He ran his fingers through her hair. "I need for you to get better, so you can be there for your daughter."

She interrupted him quick. "You mean our daughter."

"Come on, Sahara, don't do this to me."

"Don't do what? Tell the truth? Let my daughter think that her father is dead?" Sahara wiped her eyes with the hospital gown she was wearing. "You have a lot of nerve."

"How do I know that she's even mine?"

"Because I'm telling you, that's why."

"So you're saying that I need a paternity test?"

"Damn, Jayceon, nothing that comes from your mouth seems to amaze me."

"I don't want to do this. Let's just stop before its gets uglier than it already is."

"It's a little too late for that, don't you think?"

"All I'm saying is, how can I be sure?"

"You were the only other person I fucked."

116

He chimed in quickly, "Don't forget about Lock."

"I didn't fuck Lock."

"So he was lying?"

"Yes."

That was her story and she was sticking to it. She couldn't have him feeling like he didn't satisfy her.

Jayceon was not about to fight with her anymore, so he put his hands up letting her know that he surrender. "I give up."

She became defensive. "You're so quick to judge and assume the truth. Are you still fucking Tammy?"

That was the moment she had been waiting for. That was one answer that had been haunting her for over a year now and she was finally about to get an answer.

"Who?"

"Tammy."

"I don't know nobody name Tammy."

"She has a sister named Lita."

He thought long and hard, then it finally dawned on him. "I know damn well you ain't talking about Tammy with all those damn kids that lived in the projects."

"Yep."

"You got me fucked up. I wouldn't hit that hoe with somebody else's dick. Who told you that?"

"It's not important, but I heard it at the salon I go to."

He chuckled.

"What's so funny?"

"It figures my name would come up around a bunch of nosy-ass hoes."

"Did you fuck her?" she asked again.

"Man, hell no."

"So why is she spreading lies about you?"

"I don't know."

"Oh, you know, you just not telling me."

He sat up in the chair to tell her the story. "Okay, remember the apartment that I had the girls cooking dope in?"

"Yeah."

"Well, Tammy was one of the chicks that used to work in there. I used to stop by and check in on them. You know, make sure that everything was running smooth. One day she called me over and when I got there, the bitch was trying to fuck. I told her I was straight and I don't fuck with the help. After that, I stopped going over there and sent my partner instead. I guess she was mad that I turned her down."

"Yeah, okay."

"That's the truth, and you should know what type of hoes I fuck with by now. You know damn well I'm not fucking anything that looks like that."

"Yeah, I know."

"So when are you getting out of here?"

"I don't know."

"Who has the baby?"

"Kayla."

They fell silent for a little while. It was pretty clear that things had gotten awkward for them. Shit hadn't been kosher in the past twelve hours. Someone needed to break the ice.

"Do you still love me?" she asked.

"Huh?"

"Do you still love me?"

"I will always love you."

"But you're not in love with me?"

"I'm in a tough situation and you're not making this any easier for me."

"So what do you want me to do? Am I just supposed to turn my feelings off just like that?"

"Things have changed. I'm about to get married and have a baby. I have to do the right thing."

"Newsflash: you been a father." She dropped her head down low. That was the way he made her feel. "So marrying her is the right thing to do?"

"Yes. I want my kids to have a two parent home."

"What about me and your daughter? Do you even care?" she sighed in disappointment. "I can't believe that I allowed you to do this to me. I loved you wholeheartedly and you promised that you would never leave me. A bunch of broken promises is what you gave me in return."

Jayceon was tired of seeing the women that he loved cry. As soon as Sahara was out of the hospital, he was going to put an end to all of the madness and move on with his life. No more games and no more drama. In the meantime, he had to stop the one in front of him from crying. He had caused enough hurt and pain for one day, so he consoled her.

Jayceon walked over to the bed. "Sit up."

Sahara faced him with her legs dangling off the bed. He took her hands into his. "Listen, I'm sorry for all the pain that I caused you, but you have to believe me when I say my intention was never to hurt you. I loved you and all you did was push me away. I wanted to be with you, but you wouldn't leave him."

This was the first time that Jayceon ever apologized for hurting her, and it felt good to hear it. She allowed him to talk without any interruptions.

"I was selfish, and my well-being was the only thing I cared about. I know I shouldn't have walked away the way that I did. I can't change what happened back then, but I can change what happens now. I promise that I will help you get through this."

She was crying. "Don't make me promises that you can't keep. You've hurt me enough and I can't take it anymore."

For the first time in weeks, he broke his own promise and kissed her. He wasn't sure if it was the liquor or his true feelings, but he went with the flow.

Once again Sahara was weak. She had waited so long for his touch and it was finally happening. Sahara had him exactly where she wanted him, and she was going all the way. Unzipping his pants, she pulled out her old playmate and she stroked it as their tongues did the dirty wind together.

When he was rock hard, she guided him into her forbidden fruit, the one garden that he promised he would never enter again and the one garden that Cherish had forbidden him from. Jayceon pushed past her delicate petals and sank deep with no hesitation. It felt good to be back in the warmth of the walls of the woman that he would've moved a mountain for if she asked him to. He took his time going in and out of her, as if he had all the time in the world. She wrapped her legs around his waist and placed her head on his chest.

"I love you, Jayceon. Please don't let this be the end of us."

Caught up in the heat of the moment, he made the biggest mistake of saying it back. He quickly forgot that this was the door he was supposed to be closing. Instead, he made it wider. "I love you too."

Jayceon popped a breast in his mouth, sucking on her nipple with ease. Her juices coated his wood. Light squeaking echoed throughout the room. Sahara clutched the mattress and rocked her hips gracefully.

"Oh God! I missed you so much."

"Stand up." Jayceon got on his knees and slid his tongue into her budding flower. As he sucked slow and hard, she tossed one of her legs over his shoulder.

"Ooh! I needed you so bad."

He French kissed her button and squeezed her ass. "Turn over."

Sahara bent over on the bed. Jayceon eased into her nookie from behind and stroked her inner core. Reaching back, she spread one of her cheeks giving him access. Pulling out halfway, he rubbed his dick to wet his fingers. Plunging back inside, he pumped in and out while sticking his thumb in her brown eye.

"Shit!" she whispered in pleasure.

The penetration in both holes made her wetter and an orgasm was near. Biting down on her hand, she attempted to keep quiet. If a nurse walked in, she would pass the fuck out.

When she was on the verge of releasing her honey dew, so was he. Jayceon pumped harder and harder until his release. After pulling out, he bit her butt cheek and pulled his pants back up. Sahara crawled into bed while he went into the bathroom. Jayceon came back and wiped her up.

"I gotta go, but I'll see you tomorrow."

"Okay."

He kissed her on the cheek and left the room.

Jayceon had reopened the door that was partially closed and Sahara was back in love again.

After her release, she saw him for three days straight, but then he pulled a Houdini and started to ignore her calls. That sent her flying off the handle and into an evil rage. All day she sat and plotted on how to eliminate her competition.

Days later, Sahara had been dying for a chance to get revenge on Cherish, and the opportunity had finally presented itself. There was a pretty good incentive that lay ahead if she successfully completed the job. Cherish had to pay because she ruined her relationship with Jayceon and caused him to walk away from her and their daughter. So yeah, the bitch had to pay.

Sahara was dressed down in her street gear: all-black hoodie, tights, backpack, and a pair of Nikes. Oh yes, she was ready to turn his world upside down. Sahara got into her car and drove to the tax prep office that Cherish owned. It was late night, so no one was outside. Jayceon had told her before that sometimes Cherish worked late if she was really busy.

Sahara parked around the corner just to be on the safe side. To her surprise the door was unlocked, so she walked in.

"I'm sorry, but I'm closed and that door should've been locked." Cherish turned around, only to come face to face with the barrel of a gun. "Take whatever you need, just don't kill me. I'm pregnant. I have two kids and a husband, please," she pleaded with her hands up.

"Well, that's too damn bad. You took away everything that I worked so hard to keep."

"What?" Cherish was confused, but then she caught on to the voice. "Sahara?"

"Yeah, bitch, it's me. Did Jayceon tell you that he's the father of my baby?"

"No." Her body was riddled with fear.

"Humph. I figured he didn't. I wanted to tell you before I sent you away from here."

"You can have him. Just don't kill me. Don't let my kids grow up without a mother."

"Oh, they won't. They'll have me to raise them. Sweet dreams, bitch." Sahara shot Cherish twice in the stomach and started pouring gasoline over the body. Then she went to the back and worked her way to the front of the office, dousing it completely. Sahara lit some napkins and dropped them on the floor. Sahara then left the building and went back to her vehicle. As she rode past the location, a wide smile spread across her face when she saw the blazing fire.

The following morning, Jayceon showed up on Sahara's doorstep. "Well, what storm blew you this way?"

"Can I come in?"

"Sure."

"I need to crash for a few hours. Me and Cherish had a fight yesterday and I don't want to be there when she gets home."

"No problem."

The two were in bed watching television when "Breaking News" appeared across the television screen. Jayceon sat up and turned up the volume.

"*In breaking news, police have made a horrific discovery after a blazing fire has been put out. A body has been found inside this charred office behind me. The victim has been identified, but no further information will be released until the family is notified. Detectives are the death a homicide. Back to you, Gretchen.*"

Jayceon jumped from the bed in a hurry. "I gotta go."

Sahara didn't say a word. She simply rolled over and closed her eyes. She knew that he would be back later on to cry on her shoulder.

The End

BEAUTY & THE BEAST

BEAST

Rising to my feet, I grabbed my jeans that were thrown across the chair and pulled them up around my waist.

"Where are you going?" Princess asked as she rolled over to face me. "My mom won't be back until tomorrow."

"I know, but I have someplace to be in an hour."

While I continued to get dressed, she made all types of advances to get me to stay. Truly, I would have loved to stay and sleep in her love nest all day and night. But I didn't want her to think that commitment would follow. I was the true definition of a mobster and I didn't see myself fit to have a woman get inside my heart, let alone my thoughts.

Once love came, children followed, and I was not about to embed my seed into any woman. In my line of work it was smart to remain that way: no kids and no woman. Now don't get me wrong, I loved to smash on every opportunity she gave me, but to settle down with her would be uncivilized. Princess was a churchgoing female and I cherished the ground she walked on. That was why I only entertained her and no other female. She deserved that much respect, since she stuck around without a title.

The last thing I needed was for anyone to have leverage over me and make my family a target. I would paint the city red before I let that happen and that went for men, women, and children. Blind, dumb, crippled, and crazy…they were not an exemption.

"Wouldn't you like to go for round two?"

"That sounds very tempting, but I can't right now. I'll see you later." Grabbing my keys, I headed to the front door with Princess right behind me.

"I love you, Beast!"

I looked over my shoulder. "I know." And that was the reason I had to leave.

As soon as I got into the car, I called my brother, Killa. I tried his number several times, but there was no answer. Just like me, Kairu was laid to rest and Killa was born. We moved to the United States - Fort Lauderdale, to be exact - one year after the murders and spread our talents like a wildfire. One of Gitonga's closest friends helped us get established once we hit American soil. He even hooked him up with this kingpin that went by the name of Dice.

Apparently, he had prices on the heads of a few of the local hustlers and needed it taken care of immediately. Given my father's reputation and word of mouth, he immediately added him to the payroll. Although our riches were different back home, we still managed to be rich in the States as well. We managed to purchase a million dollar mansion and six foreign whips on the Inter-coastal.

Growing up, I wasn't popular with the girls until I hit my teenage years. The boys used to try me every day until I made an example out of one of them. I didn't know if it was my accent or the way I dressed that made them feel like they could try my gangster.

Killa didn't have that problem because he was still in elementary school. One day after school I was approached by this fat kid named Gary and his entourage. I knew that they were his do boys because they did everything he told them to. I witnessed that on a daily basis.

"Hey, Africa?"

Ignoring them like I normally did, I continued to walk home.

I could hear Gary tell one of his bitches to snatch my backpack. "Take it, Robert, he scared anyway."

When he snatched it, I stopped in my tracks.

"Oh, he mad now," Gary teased. "What you gon' do, put voodoo on me?"

They all started to laugh.

Being afraid was weak nigga trait, so that wasn't my reason for avoiding a conflict with his crew. What kept me quiet was the fact that I knew the damage I could cause. If he had any idea of my background, he would've sat his fat ass down somewhere. Turning around slowly, I stood toe to toe with him.

"You better walk away," I warned.

Gary started to laugh, as if I had told a joke of some sort. Then he stepped closer. "What if I don't?"

124

Balling my fists together tightly at my sides, I warned him once more. "I'm going to pummel your face in until you bleed to death."

Gary didn't believe me because I was too calm, and that was when he made the mistake of trying to sucker punch me. Quick on my feet, I ducked because I was expecting him to do that. When I came back up, I delivered several martial arts tactics that knocked him out completely.

Once he was on the ground, I punched him repeatedly in his face until it was covered in blood. His do boys were so afraid that they didn't bother to help. Instead, they ran and left him behind.

The details about the fight quickly spread across town like a sexually transmitted disease, and that was when my respect kicked in. From that day forth, everyone in my neighborhood and at school addressed me as Beast. The local gangs tried to recruit me after hearing about the damage I caused with my bare hands, but I declined all offers. They automatically assumed my hands were the reason I was given the name Beast, but little did they know they weren't even close. By the time Killa made it to middle school, he didn't have any problems, and that was based on my street credibility. Everyone was afraid to mess with the younger brother of "the beast."

When I finally made it home, to my surprise, Killa's car was in the driveway. It was only a little after one and he should've been in school. Walking straight to his bedroom, I could hear the sound of the headboard banging against the wall. Even if I didn't know what was going down, the female in the room removed all doubt. Clear as the afternoon sun, she was moaning and crying out of his name. I laughed to myself because she sounded like a virgin to me. To stir shit up a bit, I decided to go in and make my presence known.

"School is out already?" I asked while leaning against the door frame. My focus was directly on the female that was laying up under him getting the brakes knocked off.

Killa didn't bother to stop or look my way.

"Didn't you forget to knock?" He was clearly unfazed by my presence, but the girl may have been a little embarrassed. She grabbed his waist.

"Stop," she pleaded. "He's standing right there."

"Oh, that's just my brother." That was when he finally looked at me. "He's about to leave though."

Laughing out loud, I stroked my beard. "I see you found yourself a virgin?"

Killa smiled back at me. "Maybe. Now close the door. I'll be done in a few."

"I hope you wearing a condom."

Closing the door, I walked out of the room and headed down the hallway. Casually, I walked around the house to see if I could find Magda, our housekeeper. When I ran into her, she was in my sister Kainda's room.

"Magda!" I shouted.

She jumped. "Kamau, you scared me."

"I'm sorry, but could you do something for me please?"

"Sure."

"Could you make me some Samosas and bring them to my room please?"

"Of course I can."

"Thank you."

Magda was the only person that called my family by our Kenyan names, and I was okay with that. I truthfully didn't expect her to call me Beast. Magda made that known when she started working for us. On her second day, she called me Kamau and I corrected her. She kindly let me know that she was not going to be calling me a beast, or my brother a killer, for that matter. We agreed. After closing my door, I flopped down on the bed and waited on Magda to bring my food.

Saturday Night

It was my birthday, so my father threw me a big-ass mansion party on the beach. Stepping out of the stretch Hummer, I was greeted by valet and a long line of exclusive guests only. I was dressed to the nines. The women were smiling and waving, while the dudes were nodding their heads in my direction. I was dressed in a gold and black Versace bomber jacket set with the matching high top sneakers.

Around my neck was a thick Cuban link with a lion medallion that hung down to my stomach.

Turning around, I extended my hand for my date to get out. Princess stepped out matching my fly with a long, gold backless dress and strappy heels. The faces of the women changed the minute they saw who had me locked in. Princess was bad, and I wasn't the only man that thought so. I could see the hunger in their eyes as they watched my arm candy. Princess stood 5'6" with long, pure black characteristic hair that ceased at the center of her back. Her skin was dark-colored and perfect. She had light-colored, almond molded eyes, full lips, and wide hips. Her cosmetics were daintily connected, in spite of the fact that she didn't require them.

Admiring what belonged to me and no other man, I leaned closely to her ear and whispered, "You look beautiful. So don't let these niggas get you and them fucked up, okay?"

Princess giggled. "I know who I belong to. No worries."

There was no need for her to impose a similar threat. She knew that I had high standards and morals. I didn't sleep with multiple women and loved a natural woman. None of that weave and shit. It was too artificial for my taste.

I grabbed her hand and escorted her through the double glass doors. The place was laced with all-white furniture and gold accessories. Killa was standing amongst a group of his friends when we walked up.

"Happy G-Day, big bruh." He hugged me and put a black and silver box in my hand.

"What's this?"

"Open it," he insisted.

Inside was a gold Rolex watch covered in diamonds. "This is nice, but you didn't have to get me anything."

Killa snatched the box. "Just put it on."

Shaking his head, I chuckled and slipped the expensive time piece onto my arm. "You remember Princess. Don't you?"

"How could I forget such a pretty face?" He smirked while grabbing her hand and kissing it.

Moving her hand from his grip, I shook my head. Killa was clearly tipsy. "Watch it, li'l bruh. I'm bussin' heads tonight about her."

"I'm just fuckin' around."

"I know."

Princess and I went and posted up in the roped-off VIP section and sat on the sofa. The waitress on duty set a bottle of Luc Belaire Rare Rose and Hennessey in front of us. *Let the party begin!*

Princess wasn't a real fan of liquor, but she agreed to turn up with me for the occasion. Clutching her glass, she sipped on the champagne. Her classiness is what I loved the most about her. She was a twenty-one-year-old pharmaceutical student at Nova. A few months back, I bought her an Infiniti coupe when her other car gave out on her. Education was important, and I needed her to succeed. She was working at Walmart when we met. Then a few months down the line, I let her quit to focus on her studies. Our agreement was that she would receive a monthly stipend to take care of herself without the expectation of a relationship. And *no*, she wasn't allowed to date or have sex with anyone other than me. She agreed.

"Take a shot with me."

Princess took the glass from me and tossed it back. "Woo! That's strong."

"One more." I insisted.

Princess frowned and accepted. Then we took another one together.

"Can you get me a napkin?" she asked sweetly.

"Yeah. Hold on."

I stepped into the kitchen, and there were several people in there taking shots and talking shit.

One of my homies dapped me up. "This party lit, dawg."

"I'm glad you enjoying yourself."

We chopped it up for a few before I realized I had gone in there for a reason. As I stepped away and grabbed the napkin from above the sink, I was approached by a female.

"Happy birthday, handsome."

"Thank you."

"I would love to give you something for your special day."

"I'm good. Thank you."

"Oh, you're taken?"

Out of nowhere, Princess appeared and stood beside me. "You forgot my napkin."

"Sorry, love. I got sidetracked."

"I see." Princess was extremely calm.

"Oh, I'm sorry. Is this your girlfriend?"

"No."

"Hmm. So you're available to receive my gift?"

"Nah, I'm only available to one person, and this is her." Princess smiled as I whisked her away with my hand on her waist. "You handled that well."

"Yeah, it took a lot, but I know what time it is."

To clear the air, I stopped and pulled her into the hallway. There was so much noise and I didn't want to be interrupted. There was a bathroom, so we stepped inside and closed the door. "Are you upset about what I said?"

"No." she replied quickly. "I know we don't have a title."

"But what?"

Princess looked deep inside my soul with big brown eyes. "We do everything that couples do, so I don't understand why a title hasn't presented itself."

"With a title comes expectations, and I don't want to put myself in that situation. The line of work I'm in requires me to be on call day and night. I can't promise that I'll be home every day, nor I can promise that I would make it home every night. I'm great at what I do, but the sad reality is I could die on any given day and any moment."

"Don't say that."

"And that's what I'm trying to avoid."

"What? Feelings?"

"Yes. Love always gets a man killed." Princess had a sadness in her eyes, and I couldn't have that. We were supposed to be drinking and having fun. "Cheer up. You got me, and I'm not going anywhere, okay?"

"Yes."

"Now can we go back and enjoy the party?"

"Yes."

Princess and I forgot all about what we discussed. We had a few more shots and were toasted. There was no way I was leaving that night. On a search for my pops, I found him in a room gambling.

"Aye, Pops, let me holla at you real quick."

"Don't touch my muthafuckin' chips or I'll put a bullet in ya brain." Picasso walked out into the hall where Princess was standing.

"When the party over make sure you lock up."

"Where you going?"

"We headed to the master bedroom for the rest of the night."

He looked at Princess and smiled. "I see. I'm staying here tonight to keep an eye out, so enjoy."

"Okay."

Princess and I made it into the room. My clothes hit the floor as soon as I locked the door. I walked over to Princess and helped her out of her dress.

She rocked side to side. "I have to pee."

Princess darted off towards the bathroom, so I followed. Wet sex sounded good to me. Stepping into the walk-in shower, I turned the water on. The water hit both of our bodies. Princess washed her body as I copped a few feels.

The animal in me was ready to pounce all over my prey. Standing behind her, I grabbed both of her breasts and sucked on her neck. Pressing my dick against her soft booty, I pushed her against the tile wall. The liquor had me feeling like a depraved addict. Her soft, shea butter skin had me ready to lick her up and down until she begged for me to stop.

The missile poking out between my legs was ready for takeoff into her creamy universe. "Turn around."

I picked her up in my arms, put her back against the wall, and slipped inside. Careful with my strokes, I kept it nice and steady so I didn't slip and fall.

Princess sucked on my bottom lip and moaned my name several times. "Beast. Baby, I love you. God, I love you."

My mind wouldn't let my heart become weak for her. It kept my heart cold and black. However, I treated her well and respected her like the queen she was. Never would I say I loved her back. I didn't care how many times she said it. Besides, my actions spoke louder than words ever could. On God, she could have all of my possessions, but she could never have my heart. While I slid in and out of her love canal, I stroked the crack of her ass before shoving my finger inside.

Letting her down easy, I sat down on the ceramic bench and pulled her onto my lap. "Bounce on your shit."

With her back towards me, she put her hands on her knees. Princess eased down on my rod and bounced up and down on it. The sight of her butt shaking increased my appetite for affection. I wanted to make love to her. Princess stopped bouncing and grinded on my shit slow.

"Damn," I mumbled between breaths. Again, I grabbed both breasts and fondled her nipples gently.

Moving her to the bed, I laid her down and pushed her legs apart. Towering over her, I dipped inside and grinded slow. "Open up for me, queen."

"Anything for you, my king."

At a slow pace, I made sensual love to her despite the alcohol. When I hit her G-spot, she began to yodel sweetly in my ear. The snatch was extra wet and I could her gushy pulsate against my skin. Princess came long and hard, soaking the sheets. A few minutes later, every bullet that built up to my tip shot off multiple rounds into its target. That was my first time releasing my semen inside of her body.

As we cuddled, I stared up at the ceiling, thinking of nothing in particular.

Princess grabbed my jaw and turned me towards her. "You're the most intriguing man I've ever come across. Nobody has ever placed me on a pedestal the way you do. You've handled me with complete delicacy, and you've never entertained another woman. I'm confident about that. You truly treat me like a princess, yet I'm still confused about us. I need more."

"What do you want from me? I've given you almost everything. I take care of all your wants and needs."

She traced a circle around my heart. "I want this."

"You can have all of my worldly possessions. The money and cars." Then I stopped. My next words had the potential to hurt her beyond repair.

Princess's bottom lip trembled as she fought back tears that threatened to explode at any moment. "I can have everything except your heart?"

She was a damn good woman with her own morals and she would make the perfect wife, but I couldn't give her what she wanted. Emotions could never make me change my mind, but she was removing the barrier from around my heart brick by brick. No matter the circumstances, I would never reveal that delicate information.

The End

TOUCH ME, TEASE ME

Amari laid in bed, crying her eyes out and wondering how she could allow herself to fall into such a trap. Ten months ago she was happy as could be, without a single tear in sight. Suddenly everything came to an abrupt stop. Her fiancé Bullet had just been indicted on fraud charges and was facing some time. Everything they had planned was null and void and the DA was going to make sure he did some time. Amari had accepted the fact that he was definitely going away, but for how long was the question. She loved every ounce of him, but she loved herself more. After everything she had been through, Bullet finally asked for her hand in marriage. From that moment on, Amari couldn't wait to change her last name to Cash. Bullet's attorney even assured her that he wouldn't get more than two years, so what was the problem?

Six months ago she was on her way to a concert with her best friend Renee when she decided to stop for gas, and that's when he walked into her life. He pulled up behind her silver Cadillac CTS in a black Maserati with 22 inch rims and jumped out of the car as if he knew her.

"What's up, baby? How you doing?" he asked.

She could tell he was buzzed by the way he was talking. The strange thing about it was that she actually entertained it. "I'm fine. How are you?"

"Better now that I see you." He stepped in a little closer and grabbed her hand. "I like you already."

Amari pulled her hand back slowly. "You don't even know me."

He smiled. "We haven't gotten that far yet. Put your number in my phone so I can arrange that."

Amari took his phone and programmed her number. He introduced himself as Blake, and that's how it all started.

After dating Blake for six months, Amari had completely fallen for this man. He provided everything that she was missing in her own life and more. Just as soon as she thought nothing could go wrong in her perfect world, the universe showed her just how fucked up things were about to get. One day after a busy day at the pharmacy, Amari packed up her things to go home. She looked at her phone and noticed that she had three missed calls from Blake. She quickly dialed his number back, but didn't get the greeting she was looking for. It was a female.

"Who is this?" she demanded.

"Who the fuck is this?" Amari responded in shock.

"This is his wife. Now who is this?"

Everything around Amari fell silent and there was a pregnant pause. She couldn't believe her ears. "Whose wife?"

"Blake's."

"Blake ain't married. You better check that ring finger!" Amari shouted.

"This muthafucka is married, so I would advise you to not call his phone anymore." And just like that, she hung up.

Amari stared at the screen and called back as soon as she made it to her car. The phone rang until the voicemail caught it. "I don't believe this bitch."

Amari hit up her best friend Renee to come over and bring a bottle and some weed. Speeding out of the parking lot, she rushed home and got in the shower. The water soaked her naturally curly hair as she stood underneath the stream. That was her second heartbreak within a year and a half. Maybe that was her karma for not remaining faithful to Bullet while he was away. Bullet couldn't hold out on cheating while she worked a nine to five, so she didn't feel too bad about the situation.

Stepping out of the shower, she wrapped herself in a towel and went into her bedroom. Her iPhone beeped, letting her know she had missed a text. When she picked up, it was a message from Bullet, asking her to call him on video. She called him on IMO and laid in the bed.

Bullet looked rugged when he picked up. Nevertheless, he was still handsome. "Wassup, bae? What you doing?"

Amari mustered up a smile. "Just getting out the shower."

"Oooh shit. Let me see."

Flipping the screen, she gave him a full view of her caramel coated body. Since he'd been gone, Amari had put on an extra ten pounds, but her body was still banging. When she put the camera back on her face, Bullet had a huge grin on his face.

"Play with that pussy for me. My roommate left so I can have some privacy."

Amari never denied any of his requests, so she held the phone up and rubbed her fingers over her the hood of her vagina. Spreading her lips, she placed two fingers on top of her clit and stroked it in a circular motion.

"Hell yeah. Make it wet for me." Bullet was on the opposite end of the phone stroking his dick.

"Ssss. Ah! Ah!" Amari groaned while giving herself pleasure. Her eyes were clutched tight as she pictured Bullet between her legs sucking on her pearl tongue.

"That pussy look good and wet. You feel my tongue licking you up and down?"

"Yes."

"Now slide two fingers in that pussy, baby."

"Ah! I'm doing it."

"You feel this dick stroking that pussy?"

"Yes."

"Fuck them fingers, baby." Amari moved her hips against her hand. "Yeah. Yeah. That's what I'm talm 'bout. Fuck that pussy harder."

Amari moved her fingers in and out of her box fast. "You feel so good in this pussy."

"Fuck that pussy faster. You fell this dick digging in them guts?"

"Yes. Yes," she moaned. "I'm cumming."

"Come on daddy's dick."

"Okay."

"Rub that pussy on my mouth. Bounce on this tongue."

"I'm doing it. I'm doing it."

"Cum for daddy. Cum for daddy, baby."

"It's coming. It's coming." Amari's fingers were putting in work while her eyes were clenched tight.

"Daddy cumming too. I'm finna nut all up in that pussy. Squeeze yo' dick. Fuck me back."

"Shiiiitttt!" Amari screamed as she released gooey liquid on her fingers.

"I love you, baby." Bullet watched as she held her fingers in front of the screen to show her fluids. "Let me see you."

Amari flipped the screen so he could see her. "Taste that pussy. Lick them fingers clean."

Amari shoved his fingers in her mouth and moved them in and out. She missed giving him head. "Hell yeah. That was good."

She giggled. "I ain't gon' lie, it was good."

"A'ight. I'm about to hit the shower. I'll call you back later."

"Okay. Love you."

"I love you too."

Amari hung up the phone and when she looked up, Renee was standing at the threshold of her bedroom door. "Oh my goodness." She giggled. "How long have you been standing there?"

"Long enough to know that you in here having phone sex with my brother." Renee sat down on the bed and poured us up a drink. "So what's going on?"

"Why I called Blake phone today and some bitch picked up the phone claiming to be his wife?"

"Damn, for real?"

"Hell yeah. I was so mad, but it's all good. I ain't sweating that nigga. Fuck him and whoever answered his phone."

"Well, what did he say?"

"Nothing. When I called back, he didn't answer his phone."

"Leave that dumb-ass nigga alone. You shouldn't be out here stressing over no nigga. Yo' nigga in prison. This was supposed to be for entertainment, remember?"

"Thanks, Renee."

"No thanks needed."

"It is. I appreciate you keeping my secrets. I know you love your brother and how close y'all are."

"True. Bullet was doing fucked-up shit out here, so that's why I'm not going to say anything."

"Girl, I owe you big time."

"No you don't. All you have to do is keep my secret."

"What secret is that?"

"I've been crushing on you for a long time."

Her confession took Amari by surprise. Her mouth hung open as she tried to register what she just said.

That wasn't as nearly shocking as her next move though. Renee moved closer to her and kissed her on the mouth. Right when Amari was about to push her away, she put her hand between her legs and stroked her kitty. It felt good, so she held off on the interruption. Renee dipped two fingers in, penetrating her opening. The same way Bullet had her grinding on her fingers, she did the same to his sister.

Renee pushed her back on the bed and feasted on her goodies. She had her girl in a tight lip lock and it felt so good. Amari had never been with a female before, but she heard they ate pussy better than men. That assumption was beyond her, but now she had to second that. She ate Amari out with expertise.

When she was finished, Renee stood up and removed her clothes. She was a petite female with small, perky titties. "Turn on your side and lift your leg up."

Amari didn't know what the hell she was about to do to her, but she welcomed it. Renee straddled her so that their pussies were in a lip lock. Slowly she grinded her lips against Amari's. It was so erotic. Her pussy was growling every time she bumped against it. Their juices intertwined with one another and created a squishy sound. It didn't take long for Amari to reach her peak and bust all over her.

Renee laid beside her in silence. Then finally she looked over at Amari "Can you keep my secret?"

"You secret is safe with me."

They kissed, and Renee fell asleep holding Amari the same way her brother used to do.

The End

DIAMOND DICK

LEILANI

Coy had this seductive look in his eyes as he bit down on his bottom lip. That shit was so sexy to me. The cool temperature from his hand sent chills down my spine when he placed it on the back of my neck, pulling me close to him.

Our lips connected and we were engaged in a deep, intoxicating kiss. That alone was damn near erotic. I could feel his hand exploring my body slowly like he had just discovered new land. His touch alone had me weak in the knees, so I placed my hand on his thigh. Coy moved his hand from my neck, grabbed my hand and placed it between his legs. My heart stopped beating for a few seconds when I felt the size of his penis. It was hard and thick, so I drew my hand back fast. That put fear in my heart and I wasn't sure if I wanted to proceed.

Coy stopped our kiss, but he didn't move his lips from mine. "What's wrong?"

"Nothing." I lied.

"You scared?"

I swallowed hard and blinked a few times before I answered. "No." That was lie number two in less than one minute.

My inner person screamed. *Yes, bitch, we are scared. Yo' ass still a virgin.*

"Back up." Coy jumped from the dresser and placed his hands on my waist pushing me towards the bed.

When he kissed me again, it was more intense. He grabbed the bottom of my dress and tugged on it. "Take this off."

I was nervous like a hooker standing in front of a whole congregation. My hands were even shaking when I pulled the dress over my head. I dropped it to the floor and stood there in my bra and panties. His eyes roamed my body hungrily like he wanted to eat me alive.

"Damn, my baby fine. You gon' make me fuck a nigga up." I could barely laugh. My nerves were too damn shot. "Take that off too and relax." He went towards the table while I continued to undress.

Once I was naked, I climbed onto the bed and laid down on my back with my arms covering my small, perky titties. When he returned, he was holding a full glass of champagne. "Down this so you can loosen up."

I sat up and killed the whole glass with no problem and handed it back to him. "Good girl." He smiled while removing his clothing.

The waiting game was long, as I sat with anticipation for him to come out his boxers. I needed to get a good look at what I was about to get myself into. When he pulled them down I cringed. His penis was a lighter brown than his actual complexion and it had veins on it. My eyes widened at the sight. It was pretty and evenly-toned, but I didn't know how I planned on taking all of that. To keep from torturing myself, I laid back down and focused everything except Coy. I was amused at the sight of the mirror on the ceiling. I hadn't noticed that either when I walked in.

Coy climbed in between my legs and glared down at me. "You sure you wanna do this?"

"I'm sure." Coy was my man and I wanted him to be my first and only. As soon as I gave him the green light he laid flat on his stomach, pushed my legs apart and buried his head in between my thighs. The moment his lips grazed my lower region my body tensed up. He placed soft kisses on my inner thighs, teasing me. His warm, wet tongue slid up and down my center rapidly.

"Mm."

Coy put his mouth on my vagina and tongue kissed her the same way he did my other set of lips. That shit drove me wild. I found myself rocking my hips and getting into it. He sucked harder and harder like he was trying to suck my soul out my body.

"Mm." His tongue gained entrance to my opening and I could feel it slither in and out of the crease. Biting down on my clit, he nibbled on it gently with his teeth. "Ss. Mm. Oh my God!" I cried out.

My quick reflexes caused my legs to clamp themselves shut, locking down on his head. Coy rose to his knees, then placed both of his hands on my knees and pushed them up to my stomach. Head first, he shoved his tongue back inside and slurped up my juices. My legs started to shake and I could no longer keep them still.

"Ah. Ah."

I squirmed, trying to get away from his lethal tongue. That thang had me about to climb the wall. My body managed to get away from him, so he grabbed my legs and pulled me back to him.

"Stop running."

He wiped my juices from his lips and climbed on top of me. That thang was hard as a rock. The veins were thick like the lines on a Snickers bar. It was sticking straight out, pressing hard against my lips.

"We should use a condom." I was trying to tell him in so many words without directly saying it.

"I trust you. Don't you trust me?"

"You know what I mean. My daddy would kill me." I trusted him; I just didn't trust the fact that I wouldn't get pregnant during my first sexual encounter.

He leaned down and kissed me in the mouth. "I promise not to get you pregnant. I'll pull out."

"No. I'm scared." I was not trying to put myself at risk like that. College was months away and I couldn't afford to have any accidents. My father would have both of our heads on a platter.

"Trust me, baby. I'm not ready for kids either."

I was agreeing to something I knew nothing about, but I was praying that he knew what he was doing because I sure as hell didn't.

We engaged in a little more foreplay to keep me sexually aroused. Coy was a multi-tasker. He sucked and licked on my neck while rubbing my kitty to get her extra wet. I could feel the tip of his fat head pressing against me, but it wouldn't go in. I was too tight for him to just slide in, so he backed up and inserted one finger, then a second one to make it expand. My juices and his finger action started making squishy sounds.

"Yeah, she ready."

My scary ass closed my eyes quick, like that was going to help. Coy tapped his dick against my lips, then pushed past my delicate flaps to gain full access to my virgin tunnel. Thrusting against my pelvis, he broke his way through my tough barrier, tearing my hymen. My back arched to the max and a loud, piercing scream filled the room and bounced around the walls like an echo.

Coy covered my face with tender kisses while long stroking me slowly. "You okay?"

"It hurts."

Tears filled my eyes and I could no longer see a clear image of his face. Gently, he wiped away the water with his hand. My petite frame rocked along with his muscular body, making what some would call beautiful music. I wasn't there yet because every stroke made it feel like my walls were being stretched and ripped apart. So, in my mind all I heard was Freddy Krueger music. My breathing pattern was all out of whack. I was skipping beats and getting air trapped in my throat.

"Ow. Ow. Ow." My bottom lip quivered. My hands desperately searched for something to hold on to, but there was nothing there besides the sheets, so I gripped those and squeezed them tight.

"You want me to stop?"

"No." I did, but I didn't want him to see me as a little girl. All I wanted was for the pain to subside. I lifted my legs and I could feel something warm run down my thigh. It felt sticky when his pelvis touched mine. I ignored it and locked my legs onto his. My pussy muscles had his dick gripped tight causing heavy friction down there. The sheets weren't helping at all. I needed something else to grab, and his body was my only option. His head was buried deep into my neck, sucking on my hot spot and playing with my erect nipples.

Coy's pushed in to me slowly and his rod went deeper, sinking into corners I didn't know existed until now. The deeper he went, the further my nails sank into his back.

"Ahh. Baby. Coy. Please." My words were all gibberish.

My eyes zoomed in on the mirror mounted against the ceiling. Being able to see him move and grind on top of my body was something I couldn't explain. It took me to a different place, my early teenage years, which allowed me to forget about the pain for a little while.

142

"Let's make a pact, Leilani: that we will lose our virginity together." Caussia suggested while we were sitting on the front porch engaging in girl talk.

"I don't know how that's going to play out, but we can try." We picked up our soda cans, clinked them together and took a sip. *"And for the record, whoever I lose my virginity to, we are getting married.*

And I still felt that way.

The sound of our skin slapping erupted and brought me back to reality when he drilled me without warning. I tried holding onto him tight in an effort to slow him down, but that didn't work. He kept on pounding away at my box. My insides felt like they were in fire.

"Ow! Ow! Slow down." It sounded like I was yodeling. Right away he slowed down and handled my body just the way I wanted him to. After a while the shot of champagne took effect, easing the pain just a little. So it didn't hurt too badly.

"I wanna hold you," he whispered.

That blew me because I didn't know what he was talking about. "What you mean?"

"I'll show you. Get up."

Coy got up, sat on the edge of the bed and planted his feet on the floor. "Come sit in my lap."

In my heart, I wasn't ready to try new positions, but I also couldn't turn him down, even though my pussy was aching. Just when I was about to straddle him, I caught a glimpse of some blood between his legs and mine, so I paused in front of him.

"Don't worry about it; that's natural." He was trying to school me. After all, he had more experience than I did.

I took his word for it and eased down onto his dick slowly. My walls stretched slowly and adjusted to the thickness of the base, filling me up and fitting him tight like a glove. It wasn't all the way in, so with a little assistance Coy slipped his arms underneath mine, bringing his hands on my shoulders and pulled me down forcibly onto him. I yelped out in pain.

"Ahhh. That hurts."

"Just relax and wrap your legs around my waist."

I did as I was told even though it was uncomfortable and let Coy take control of what was to happen next.

As promised, he held me tight and rocked my body on top of his at a steady pace. We remained upright on the edge of the bed as our bodies grinded back and forth on one accord. After a few minutes of being extra, I was finally able to relax, and we were able to make some beautiful music.

My lips grazed his in the midst of me panting, our tongues interlocked and things grew intense quickly. I kissed him harder and sucked his tongue all while caressing his body. The sound of Kut Klose's "I Like" played softly in the background.

Tender lovin', its one on one
Don't want to rush it, nah
Lets take it nice n slow, honey
Caress my body, and hold me tight...

Everything about the sex was sensual. I didn't feel rushed and he took his time with my body and made sure I was satisfied. For sure my neck was going to have so many hickeys because he couldn't keep his mouth and tongue off my body. There was no hiding that.

"Ooh. Mm. Mm." I moaned. "I love you so much." A lone tear escaped my eye the minute I said those words.

"I love you too, baby."

My insides started to contract and vibrate while I rode him with guidance. I didn't know what was happening, but I wasn't about to stop it. This experience had me feeling shit I never felt before. After a few more strokes, I couldn't hold it any longer. "I have to pee," I moaned in his ear.

"That's not pee. You about to nut and so am I." Coy gripped my booty cheeks, forcing me to bounce up and down on his dick.

"I can feel it. Don't hold it?"

"Nah, cream all over this dick."

The banging was harder and harder, so I bit down on his neck to take my mind off of my own pain. He had my pussy in flames and I wanted to scream, but I was having mixed emotions. It hurt, but at the same time it felt good. There was an eruption inside of me and my soul begin to cry, flooding him with vaginal tears. That was an experience I definitely wanted to feel again.

Coy started to breath hard. "Shit. Shit. Ooh. Fuck." He grunted. The noises continued for another minute. "Ooh, I'm finna nut in this pussy. Shit." I was caught up in the moment that I ignored the words that came from his mouth. "I'm puttin' a baby in yo' ass."

The grip he had on my shoulders became tighter with every thrust. "You gon' have my baby?"

"I can't," I whimpered into his ear.

"That's the wrong answer." Coy raised up with me in my arms and laid me down on my back with his dick still in me. He raised my leg, leaned in close to my body and dug deep into my pussy, causing me to scream.

"Ouuu!" I shouted like I was catching the Holy Ghost. "Coy, it hurts."

"I ain't stopping until you say it."

The power of the stroke had me saying anything. He was killing me, and I couldn't hold out any longer. I needed a break and some water, so I gave up.

"Okay. Okay!" I cried.

"Okay what?" he grunted.

"I'll have your baby." I didn't mean it, I just wanted him to stop.

Coy's body jerked a few times, as he sunk deeper and deeper into my walls. He was completely drenched in sweat. "I'm coming for real this time. Be still."

I just laid there and waited on him to finish and when he was done he laid down beside me.

"Damn you gone have a nigga sprung." I moved closer to him and laid my head on his chest, while we took a few moments to catch our breath.

"Me too." I agreed.

The next day I met up with my girl Caussia to fill her in on all the details. We sat on her porch while I gave her an earful. "Bitch, I want every single detail. Do he eat pussy? Ass? Can he fuck?"

Her excitement was enough to make me laugh. "Shut up, so I can tell you fool. You more excited than me."

"That's a lie. I know you happy."

"He does eat pussy. I don't know about ass 'cause he didn't do it and he had me climbing the walls all night."

"Awww bestie not a virgin anymore. I'm so proud of you." Caussia sucked her teeth. "Cause I was starting to think that you were gonna die a damn virgin."

"Nope, but I do think I might be a little sprung now."

"Well damn, bitch. Did he suck your soul out your pussy too?"

"That's what it felt like." Just thinking about Coy had me cheesing. "I need you to lie for me."

"About?"

"I can't stay out overnight because my dad was pretty pissed about me coming home this afternoon. You have to tell him that I'm here if he calls. I told him that I'm spending the night over here."

"Girl, your daddy ain't dumb. I'll do though. It's hard to trick that old school-ass nigga."

We giggled and I told her all about my first time. Every single detail. A few hours later I was on my way to Coy's apartment. What went down last night, had to happen again. Caussia told me that once I got my first piece of dick, I would feening for it. She was right because the seat of my panties were moist and hotter than a Florida summer.

The End

Here's a sneak peek of: Corrupted by a Gangsta, which is available on Amazon now for purchase….

BRICK

Dead and drunk weight was the devil, 'cause ain't no way in hell this woman was supposed to be this heavy. Her ass didn't feel like this when I was beating her down in the shower. Zuri was knocked out as soon as I put her in the car. She was even snoring lightly. It was all good; she was still cute. Instead of going back to her place, I decided to take her back to mine. That should give her some security that I had nothing to hide, and my intentions with her were genuine.

Her girl, Kyra, was low-key pissed and eyeing a nigga with dirty looks in the parking lot 'cause she was trying to get at me hard in the club, but I brushed her off and put Gucci on her ass. She saw my hand under Zuri's dress rubbing on her ass, so I blew her a kiss to fuck with her head.

Waking her up so she could walk on her own was a damn struggle. I don't know why I let her mix her liquor. I had her ass fucked up. That's what my ass gets, because I ended up having to carry her upstairs. I was thankful for the elevator. When I got to the front door, I had to throw her over my shoulder so I could get my keys out of my pocket and unlock the door. The light from the kitchen was still on, so that made it easier to walk through without tripping over the duffle bag I left on the floor.

When I got to the bedroom and laid her in the middle of my California king bed, I was relieved. A nigga was too tipsy for all that extra shit, but I had to carry my baby since she was tapped out. One by one, I removed her heels and dropped them onto the floor. I knew for a fact them dogs was barking in them high-ass shoes. No one could make me understand why women went through so much pain just to be cute. For good measure, I massaged both of her feet, only 'cause they were pretty. If she had those *Twelve Years a Slave* feet, her ass would've been up shit creek with no paddle and she would've woke up with socks on. As I caressed each foot she became more relaxed, so she had to be enjoying it. Zuri moved her leg closer to her body, giving me a clear shot of her pretty hairless pussy. I couldn't help but sing "Ms. Pretty Pussy" by Plies.

"Ms. Pretty Pussy, she can get it hot and gushy. Ms. Pretty Pussy, I like the way you twerk it for me."

My dick was getting hard just by looking at it. I already knew it was good. Now I needed to know if it tasted as good as it looked. My mouth watered like this was my first meal in the real world. One leg was already open, so I pushed open the other one and ran my finger over her clit in a circular motion. While a nigga was locked up, I used to dream about devouring some cat when I touched down, but since I didn't trust Deja's funky ass, I waited. Regardless of the way I met Zuri and the short amount of time we'd known each other, I trusted her, so I didn't have a problem smashing her raw or eating the twat.

Ready to dive in, I got down to her level and inhaled her scent. That shit smelled like water - no smell at all. *Oh yeah, she edible!* Using my thumbs to spread her lips open, I slid my tongue across her opening. That thang was pink like cotton candy, sweet like it too. I flicked my tongue up and down like my shit was a paintbrush. Zuri squirmed in her sleep and a slight moan escaped those soft-ass lips. Her eyes fluttered when I nibbled on her little man in a boat. "Mmm. Sss," she sounded like a snake.

That thang was juicy like a mango as I slurped and suctioned on it like I was trying to make it dry. Her eyes finally opened, catching a glance at me in action. My tongue was fat, so I made sure I hit every corner. I inserted two fingers inside, flexing them in the *come here* motion, in search of that G-spot.

"Ahh." She bit down on her lip. "Ooh. What you doing to me?"

Her question didn't warrant answering, so I kept at what I was doing, sucking and finger fucking her at the same time.

"Cum for me, beautiful." My mouth was full, but I could still make my demands.

"Ahh. I'm trying." Her moans were sexy as hell and music to my ears. She closed her eyes, but I wasn't having that shit. Not tonight. I stopped munching on her goodies and pulled her roughly to the edge of the bed.

"Try harder." I nudged her leg with my elbow. "Spread your legs wide and keep 'em open."

Zuri grabbed her ankles, then I shoved three fingers inside her warm pussy pool. After I found that spot, I curled my fingers and let them do the talking. They were saying, *bring that pussy here, girl.* Zuri was trying to hold in that noise, but I needed to hear it loud like some Beats by Dre. Aggressively and quickly, I moved my hand from side to side, hitting that erotic spot again.

"Oooooh, shit!" she screamed. "Baby, I can feel it coming. Keep going. Don't stop."

"That's what I'm lookin' fa."

My fingers stabbed her deep and hard, constantly hitting that spot for minutes on end, but I wasn't stopping until I got the results I was looking for. Zuri's screams were loud, yet filled with so much pleasure. I was getting off just by watching her buck in bed like she was having a damn seizure.

"Cum for me, baby." My voice was deep as I coached her right to an orgasm. Her juices leaked slowly, before shooting out and squirting like a fountain. Her eyes widened in amusement.

"Hell, yeah. Let it go." My fingers kept working until the squirting stopped. Her breathing was all off-key, like she needed an oxygen tank. I pulled my fingers out and rubbed her lips. She was hesitant, but all that was about to change.

"You scared to taste yourself?" I licked one of my fingers first, then placed them into her mouth. "I'm a freak, so you might as well get used to this. That's your first time squirting?"

She nodded her head yes.

My dick was on swole and so ready to dig in some guts, I couldn't get naked fast enough. I pulled her back to the edge of the bed, pushed her knees up to her shoulders and dropped that dick right in her.

"Grrr," I grunted when I felt her shit grip my piece tight like a vice grip. It was so tight and wet. "Ooh, shit."

"Oww," she moaned, placing her hands and feet on my chest trying to push me up out of it. I put my hands on her thighs to hold them down, applying pressure so I could put every inch in there. I wanted to see that stomach rise and fall when I went balls deep in it.

"Sss. Oww."

She kept moving and squirming and wouldn't stop until I finally let go. Grabbing her legs, I held them in the air and grinded slowly against her center, hitting every corner.

"Shit." I loved to see her lips grip my shit like she be doing her Kegels every day. Zuri had to have a snapper, 'cause I swear it felt like that bitch was biting my meat in there. Finally dropping her legs, I took a few deep strokes and that made her sit up and grab my neck. "Ooh!" she cried, "You killin' me."

I scooped her up and beat that pussy midair, instant replay of the shower scene. That only lasted for so long before it slipped out. I didn't know how flexible she was, but I was about to find out. I let her down, so she could stand up. Grabbing her leg, I raised it just enough to slide my dick back inside and raised that muthafucka to my shoulder. My grip was tight on her thigh while I pounded away. This time, I wasn't stopping until I busted a nut. From time to time, I smacked her ass, making it clap. By the time I finished punishing her, my neighbors were gonna know my name like Trey Songz. Zuri didn't know if she wanted to call me Brick or Brandon. To me, it didn't matter which one she chose. She had permission to call me by my government name.

Zuri managed to stay in that position without fighting me for about ten minutes, before I let loose, glazing her walls with my fluids.

***

The following morning, I stirred in my sleep from having a good-ass dream. I didn't want to get up, but I felt this warm and wet sensation below my waist. Last night was wild, but I wasn't that far gone to be pissing on my expensive-ass sheets. When I found the strength to open up my eyes, Zuri was face down in my lap, giving me the wettest sloppy toppy. To see my piece going in and out of her mouth was a beautiful sight. Her lips were wrapped around the python extra tight, like she was trying to tame him or pull the skin off.

"Damn, this how you wake yo' man up in the mornings?" Her eyes landed on mine for a brief second to nod her head before going back to bobbing and weaving. "Shit," I coughed, getting my words stuck in my throat. I guided her head to guide her pace.

Zuri slurped and licked on the tip while jacking me off slowly until she took me back into her mouth, making it disappear inch by inch. The tip of my head hit the back of her throat and she did some shit with her muscles that massaged it tight. It made me nut the fuck up, especially when she squeezed my balls at the same time. My damn toes were Crip walking in my socks.

"Damn, girl. Fuck." Her ass had me moaning like a bitch, no matter how hard I was trying to suppress it. My fingers were massaging the shit out her scalp.

Zuri's head moved rapidly up and down, suctioning the shaft like a vacuum. A tingling sensation arose from my nut sack, traveling all the way up. The sudden urge to thrust my pelvis hit me hard, so I grabbed her head and pushed her down further to meet me halfway.

"Ohh, shit," I gasped. "I'm 'bout ta nut."

Every thrust was on a steady beat. My dick and her mouth were having crazy sex. All of my concentration was on busting, so I closed my eyes until I started shooting off in her mouth.

"It's coming. Shit. Ahh." That didn't stop Zuri from shining me up, but my shit was sensitive. I tried to move her head, but she had me on lock in her jaws. That was making me crazy.

"Baby, baby, baby, please, stop," I begged. My knees never buckled while I was on my back. Oh yeah, she *wifey!* Big facts.

Zuri released the hold she had on me and I was finally able to breathe. "Whoo!" I exhaled.

She laughed and crawled beside me, laying in the crease of my arm. "You sound like a girl."

"You tryin' to kill a nigga?"

"That was payback from last night when you almost killed me."

"Bruh, I knew that's what you was doing. You nasty for that."

"I'm nasty?" She raised that fat head of hers. "I don't think so. Do you remember what you did to me? I almost lost my voice messing with you."

"Almost doesn't count and that ain't fair, 'cause I was asleep."

"Well, favor ain't fair."

There was something about the woman in my bed that made me want her beyond sex. Her lips were calling my name, so I pulled her closer in order to taste them. My tongue found hers and kissed her sloppily. Shorty had that effect on me and that was real talk. Before it was all said and done, she was gone be mine.

"See how I kissed you in the mouth with no problem after you sucked my dick?"

Zuri frowned and poked her lips out. "Why so vulgar?"

"I'm sorry, baby. Let me start over." I was trying my best to keep from laughing, 'cause she was legit pouting over that comment. "Do you see how I kissed you in the mouth after you rocked my mic?"

"Now you being funny." She slapped my arm.

"Nah." I flipped on my side so we could see each other face-to-face. "Don't be offended. I was only joking and besides, I love to see those pretty lips wrapped around my, you know what."

"Yeah, I bet."

"I'm a bonafide freak. In due time, you will get used to it after I turn you into one."

"In due time, huh?"

Being slow wasn't my specialty, but I was sensing a little attitude. I just didn't know if she was serious or playing. "Why you gotta say it like that?"

"Honestly, I didn't think anything would come from this. After we did what we did, you just up and left like it was nothing to you. I mean, you didn't say bye, you didn't leave a number or come back later, so I felt like it was just a fuck and that I needed to get over it. Then, my gullible ass sees you again after I thought I wouldn't and fell back into the same trap again, getting drunk and fucked, knowing damn well the same thing gone happen again."

The words she spit at a nigga had me a little heated after catching me off guard, but I knew I needed to evaluate my response before I said it. Instead of snapping, I put myself in her shoes.

"Okay, I deserve that, but believe me when I say it ain't like that, so you ain't gotta come at a nigga sideways. The way we met was just so flat out crazy and unexpected. I'm still trying to wrap my head around it. Since that day, I had been contemplating how to approach you, because I wanted my second approach to trump the first one. But we ended up running into each other last night, and here we are again, and that wasn't a coincidence. I don't believe in that bullshit."

"All of that sounds good, but we both know why I'm here. We were both drunk, and that led up to us fucking. But the fact of the matter is, I opened my home up to you and my legs, and you didn't have the decency to say nothing to me and you probably still wouldn't have if you didn't see me. That's just how I feel. I'm just somebody to fuck, and that's why you brought me here."

Now, that shit blew a nigga, knocking me clean off my muthafuckin' rocker. I eased up from the bed. This girl was pissing me off and I had a bad temper that she knew nothing about. The shit Zuri witnessed when we met was only a sample - empty threats since I wasn't going to hurt her as long as she followed my instructions. Shit could get worse and I swear she didn't want to be a victim to these hands. I could damage her in more ways than one. I glared down at her with piercing eyes and bit down on my bottom lip.

"I'm sayin' though, if you feel like a nigga only wanna fuck, why the fuck you still here? I ain't kidnap yo' ass this time, and you here, so you'll know where I live and to show you I have nothing to hide from you. A nigga ain't hard up for no pussy. I can get any bitch in Lauderdale to fuck and suck this dick, so don't get that shit twisted. In case you didn't know, I'm that nigga, so do your homework before you come at me like I'm some elementary school fuck nigga."

Zuri didn't know who she was fuckin' with and she didn't know how heavy my name was in these streets. Her ass better check my goddamn resume, 'cause I don't fuck off, point blank period. I walked off on her ass and went to the bathroom. All the liquor I consumed the night before was ready to come out. I stood over the toilet and took a long piss like a race horse and washed my hands. When I went back into the room, she was getting dressed. If she wanted to leave, I wasn't gon' stop her. Maybe it wasn't destiny after all. There was sadness in her eyes, but I didn't give a fuck. Her slick-mouth ass tried me hard.

After putting on her dress, she came to my side of the bed, brushing past me and looking for her shoes and car keys. Once they were in her hands, she hauled ass in the direction of the door. I strolled behind her since I was in no rush and had no intention on walking her downstairs. Shit was going good and she just went flip mode on me for no reason. That's 'cause she was used to fuckin' wit' these lame-ass niggas, the complete opposite of me. Females like that didn't know how to act when a boss graced them with their presence.

Zuri unlocked my door and snatched it open, slamming it behind her.

Boom!

She ain't tell a nigga bye or nothing. *What kind of shit was that?* If I was in the mood for the drama, I would've chased her downstairs and showed her what time it was. It was cool. She got a pass on that one.

The End

Don't stop just yet….

For the full story of Diamond Dick with Leilani and Coy, head over to Amazon and purchase the standalone novel titled, *Blinded by his Love*.

Also, follow me on social media and be on the lookout for full length novels from the following short stories…

Beauty & the Beast

Thug Luvin'

Cum For Me 5

For the Love of a Thug

COMING SOON!!

Gunz & Blaze: His Bonnie, Her Clyde

Foreign & Domestic: The Price You Pay for Love

She Can't Have You

Married to a Cartel Princess

Destiny Skai

Submission Guideline

Submit the first three chapters of your completed manuscript to ldpsubmissions@gmail.com, subject line: Your book's title. The manuscript must be in a .doc file and sent as an attachment. Document should be in Times New Roman, double spaced and in size 12 font. Also, provide your synopsis and full contact information. If sending multiple submissions, they must each be in a separate email.

Have a story but no way to send it electronically? You can still submit to LDP/Ca$h Presents. Send in the first three chapters, written or typed, of your completed manuscript to:

LDP: Submissions Dept
Po Box 870494
Mesquite, Tx 75187

DO NOT send original manuscript. Must be a duplicate.

Provide your synopsis and a cover letter containing your full contact information.

Thanks for considering LDP and Ca$h Presents.

Destiny Skai

BAE BELONGS TO ME III
SOUL OF A MONSTER II
By **Aryanna**
THE COST OF LOYALTY **III**
By **Kweli**
SHE FELL IN LOVE WITH A REAL ONE **II**
By **Tamara Butler**
RENEGADE BOYS **III**
By **Meesha**
A GANGSTER'S SYN II
By **J-Blunt**
KING OF NEW YORK V
RISE TO POWER III
COKE KINGS III
By **T.J. Edwards**
GORILLAZ IN THE BAY III
De'Kari
THE STREETS ARE CALLING II
Duquie Wilson
KINGPIN KILLAZ IV
STREET KINGS 2
PAID IN BLOOD 2
Hood Rich
SINS OF A HUSTLA II
ASAD
TRIGGADALE III
Elijah R. Freeman
MARRIED TO A BOSS III
By Destiny Skai & Chris Green

158

KINGZ OF THE GAME III

Playa Ray

SLAUGHTER GANG II

By Willie Slaughter

THE HEART OF A SAVAGE II

By Jibril Williams

FUK SHYT II

By Blakk Diamond

THE DOPEMAN'S BODYGAURD II

By Tranay Adams

Available Now

RESTRAINING ORDER **I & II**

By **CA$H & Coffee**

LOVE KNOWS NO BOUNDARIES **I II & III**

By **Coffee**

RAISED AS A GOON I, II, III & IV

BRED BY THE SLUMS I, II, III

BLAST FOR ME I & II

ROTTEN TO THE CORE I II III

A BRONX TALE I, II, III

DUFFEL BAG CARTEL I II III

By **Ghost**

LAY IT DOWN **I & II**

LAST OF A DYING BREED

BLOOD STAINS OF A SHOTTA I & II

By **Jamaica**

LOYAL TO THE GAME

LOYAL TO THE GAME II

LOYAL TO THE GAME III

LIFE OF SIN I, II

By **TJ & Jelissa**

BLOODY COMMAS I & II

SKI MASK CARTEL I II & III

KING OF NEW YORK I II,III IV

RISE TO POWER I II

COKE KINGS I II

By **T.J. Edwards**

IF LOVING HIM IS WRONG…I & II

LOVE ME EVEN WHEN IT HURTS I II

By **Jelissa**

WHEN THE STREETS CLAP BACK I & II III

By **Jibril Williams**

A DISTINGUISHED THUG STOLE MY HEART I II & III

LOVE SHOULDN'T HURT I II III IV

RENEGADE BOYS I & II

By **Meesha**

A GANGSTER'S CODE I &, II III

A GANGSTER'S SYN

By **J-Blunt**

PUSH IT TO THE LIMIT

By **Bre' Hayes**

BLOOD OF A BOSS **I, II, III, IV, V**

By **Askari**

THE STREETS BLEED MURDER **I, II & III**

THE HEART OF A GANGSTA I II& III

By **Jerry Jackson**

CUM FOR ME

CUM FOR ME 2

CUM FOR ME 3

CUM FOR ME 4

CUM FOR ME 5

An **LDP Erotica Collaboration**

BRIDE OF A HUSTLA **I II & II**

THE FETTI GIRLS **I, II& III**

CORRUPTED BY A GANGSTA I, II III, IV

By **Destiny Skai**

WHEN A GOOD GIRL GOES BAD

By **Adrienne**

THE COST OF LOYALTY

By Kweli

A GANGSTER'S REVENGE **I II III & IV**

THE BOSS MAN'S DAUGHTERS

THE BOSS MAN'S DAUGHTERS II

THE BOSSMAN'S DAUGHTERS III

THE BOSSMAN'S DAUGHTERS IV

THE BOSS MAN'S DAUGHTERS **V**

A SAVAGE LOVE **I & II**

BAE BELONGS TO ME I II

A HUSTLER'S DECEIT I, II, III

WHAT BAD BITCHES DO I, II, III

SOUL OF A MONSTER

By **Aryanna**

A KINGPIN'S AMBITON

A KINGPIN'S AMBITION **II**

I MURDER FOR THE DOUGH

By **Ambitious**

TRUE SAVAGE

TRUE SAVAGE II

TRUE SAVAGE **III**

TRUE SAVAGE **IV**

TRUE SAVAGE **V**

TRUE SAVAGE **VI**

By **Chris Green**

A DOPEBOY'S PRAYER

By **Eddie "Wolf" Lee**

THE KING CARTEL **I, II & III**

By **Frank Gresham**

THESE NIGGAS AIN'T LOYAL **I, II & III**

By **Nikki Tee**

GANGSTA SHYT **I II &III**

By **CATO**

THE ULTIMATE BETRAYAL

By **Phoenix**

BOSS'N UP **I , II & III**

By **Royal Nicole**

I LOVE YOU TO DEATH

By Destiny J

I RIDE FOR MY HITTA

I STILL RIDE FOR MY HITTA

By **Misty Holt**

LOVE & CHASIN' PAPER

By **Qay Crockett**

TO DIE IN VAIN

SINS OF A HUSTLA

By **ASAD**

BROOKLYN HUSTLAZ

By **Boogsy Morina**

BROOKLYN ON LOCK I & II

By **Sonovia**

GANGSTA CITY

By **Teddy Duke**

A DRUG KING AND HIS DIAMOND I & II III

A DOPEMAN'S RICHES

HER MAN, MINE'S TOO I, II

CASH MONEY HO'S

By Nicole Goosby

TRAPHOUSE KING **I II & III**

KINGPIN KILLAZ I II III

STREET KINGS

PAID IN BLOOD

By **Hood Rich**

LIPSTICK KILLAH **I, II, III**

CRIME OF PASSION I & II

By **Mimi**

STEADY MOBBN' **I, II, III**

By **Marcellus Allen**

WHO SHOT YA **I, II, III**

Renta

GORILLAZ IN THE BAY **I II**

DE'KARI

TRIGGADALE I II

Elijah R. Freeman

GOD BLESS THE TRAPPERS I, II, III

THESE SCANDALOUS STREETS I, II, III

FEAR MY GANGSTA I, II, III

THESE STREETS DON'T LOVE NOBODY I, II

BURY ME A G I, II, III, IV, V

A GANGSTA'S EMPIRE I, II, III, IV

THE DOPEMAN'S BODYGAURD

Tranay Adams

THE STREETS ARE CALLING

Duquie Wilson

MARRIED TO A BOSS... I II

By Destiny Skai & Chris Green

KINGZ OF THE GAME I II

Playa Ray

SLAUGHTER GANG II

By Willie Slaughter

THE HEART OF A SAVAGE

By Jibril Williams

FUK SHYT

By Blakk Diamond

BOOKS BY LDP'S CEO, CA$H

TRUST IN NO MAN

TRUST IN NO MAN 2

TRUST IN NO MAN 3

BONDED BY BLOOD

SHORTY GOT A THUG

THUGS CRY

THUGS CRY 2

THUGS CRY 3

TRUST NO BITCH

TRUST NO BITCH 2

TRUST NO BITCH 3

TIL MY CASKET DROPS

RESTRAINING ORDER

RESTRAINING ORDER 2

IN LOVE WITH A CONVICT

Coming Soon

BONDED BY BLOOD 2

BOW DOWN TO MY GANGSTA

www.ingramcontent.com/pod-product-compliance
Lightning Source LLC
Chambersburg PA
CBHW060419260626
47161CB00005B/1700